I0760708

Glass Kingdom

M. Lynn

Fantasy and Fairytales

Edited by Melissa Craven
Proofread by Patrick Hodges
Cover by Covers by Combs

Also by M. Lynn

Fantasy and Fairytales

Golden Curse

Golden Chains

Golden Crown

Glass Kingdom

Glass Princess

Noble Thief

Cursed Beauty

The Hidden Warrior

Dragon Rising

Dragon Rebellion

Queens of the Fae

Fae's Deception

Fae's Defiance

Fae's Destruction

Fae's Prisoner

Fae's Power

Fae's Promise

Legacy of Light

A War for Magic

A War for Truth

A War for Love

For Bri,

the first person who told me I should publish all those years ago. Your support and friendship has pushed me. We've come a long way together and we have a long way yet to go.

The Six Kingdoms

One

One day, when trying to remember the first time she'd seen him, Helena would think of the energy sparking in the air around him.

The unknown boy should have been no match for the broad man before him, yet the crowd cheered as if the fight would go on forever.

Boxing was a revered sport on the coast of Madra. Not that her parents had ever allowed Helena to attend a match.

But this wasn't an organized fight. There was no arena surrounding them, only a circle of onlookers. Their noise had drawn the small-framed girl dressed in her brother's clothing.

Helena pulled the cap on her head down over her ears to further hide the ebony locks pinned underneath.

There were two rules in Madran boxing. Never step out of bounds and never use the heel of your hand. Everything else was fair game.

The boy with lively blue eyes ducked an oncoming

punch, but didn't move quickly enough and his opponent's fist grazed the side of his head. He reeled back, stumbling before dropping to his knees.

The bigger man moved to strike again, and the boy fell sideways only to receive a kick to the abdomen.

Helena's stomach roiled. She wanted to scream, to tell them to stop, but a hand clenched around her arm.

"Princess," a low voice said in her ear. "Do not say a word."

Fear ripped into her until the man holding her pushed back his hood, revealing a head of blonde hair and a scowl only reserved for her.

"Let me go, Edmund."

"I will release you, but you aren't to leave." He lifted his hand, watching her for any sign she'd bolt. When she stayed, he turned his attention to the oversized man who continued to brutalize the smaller man.

Edmund walked forward and pushed aside his cloak, revealing a sword. The attacker froze.

"Orlo." Edmund's voice was calm, but Helena detected the ice in his words. "Challenging children to fights now?"

Helena winced at the children remark. The boy looked no younger than her eighteen years. When Edmund first arrived at their shores, she'd been smitten with him. Then she got to know the oaf, and he became just another one of her brothers.

Orlo grunted and wiped his bloody knuckles on his pants. "This 'kid' needs to learn respect."

Edmund made a sound in the back of his throat. "You know as well as I that whatever Dell did won't be anywhere near your punishment for fighting outside a proper match." He jerked his head. "Go, and I won't report this incident to the king… or the priesthood."

Fear sparked in Orlo's eyes at the mention of the order. No one in Madra wanted to face the white-cloaked lawmakers and their prison cells. Orlo didn't hesitate to run once given the chance.

"How do you expect to keep this from father?" Helena asked. "They were in the middle of the city." She threw a nervous look over her shoulder. "You know as well as I the priesthood has eyes everywhere."

Edmund walked toward the boy who must have been Dell and bent down. "Your father and his dogs will hear of this alright. But you don't understand this city, Len. There isn't a single person who will turn Orlo or Dell over for questioning." He placed two fingers against the boy's neck. "Well, he's alive, so there's that at least." Blowing the hair out of his face, he straightened and glanced around at the gathering crowd. "Don't you have better things to do?"

He shook his head as they scattered and then turned to Helena. "You and I will have words once Dell is tended to." He hefted Dell onto his shoulder as if he weighed nothing. "Come."

She ran to keep up with Edmund's long strides. He led her through the crowded city as if he'd lived there his entire life. In reality, he'd only been in Madra for the past two years, serving as the ambassador from Bela. There were rumors winding their way through the palace about Edmund and his relationship to the queen and king of Bela. Some said they were close, others spoke of imprisonments. Each story ended with Edmund requesting an assignment far from the kingdom he'd fought a war to save.

Helena wasn't complaining though. She had four brothers, but none understood her as much as Edmund.

"Edmund," she started. She needed to explain her presence in the city. It was forbidden by the laws and traditions of Madra for a princess to leave the walls of the palace unaccompanied and unmasked.

"Not here." He turned into a narrow alley running between two pale-brick buildings, leading to a busy street.

Curious Madran eyes followed them, but Edmund was well known, and most feared to be in his presence. Those stories from the palace? They also spoke of his magic. Something Helena had never seen and had trouble believing existed.

Two years ago, Madran troops were sent to aid the Belaen queen in her war against La Dame. Persinette Basile took her kingdom back and those Madran troops who fought by her side came home with the most marvelous tales of magic. The minstrels, fascinated with their tall tales of magic and spells, turned the soldiers' stories of the Belaen queen into epic songs.

Even the mercenaries who'd fought with Dracon against the royal Madran forces had their share of tales for anyone brave enough to approach them.

Belaens. Draconians. They were all feared for what they could do. Madran mercenaries were feared for who they were. Righteous bastards with loyalty to no crown. They pledged allegiance to one thing: gold. Was this Dell one of them? One of those causing trouble in the streets of Madra?

The priesthood worked to expel all mercenaries from the city, but occasionally a few would appear in the taverns or among the seedier shops on the outskirts of the city. Helena scanned her surroundings as Edmund led her between those shops.

Edmund ducked into a doorway at the end of the square and ushered Helena in before closing the heavy wooden door, shutting out all sunlight.

Small candles along one wall gave the only hint of light. If it weren't for the tendrils of cinnamon floating through the air, Helena would have suspected he'd led her into a tomb.

Edmund lifted a hand and the flames on the candles grew larger.

"Did you do that?" Her eyes rounded, fear gripping her chest as she took a step back.

Edmund ignored her. "Mari," he called, charging toward an open door. "Mari, we need you and Corban."

A middle-aged woman with deep lines in her face appeared in the doorway, took one look at Dell, and pointed to a bed on the far wall.

Edmund set him down as a young boy skipped into the room. He froze when he saw them.

Mari's warm eyes gazed at the child. "We need you, Corban."

Corban shook his head and glanced at Helena.

Edmund stepped forward. "It's okay. He's a friend."

It took Helena a moment to realize he meant her. She was still disguised in her brother's clothes. These people couldn't find out who she was no matter how much Edmund trusted them.

She only nodded, deciding that speaking would give her away.

Corban sighed.

Mari ran a hand over the top of the boy's head. "He's worried. Magic might not be outlawed in Madra as it once was in Gaule, but the fear still exists within the city. If word got out… we don't know what would happen to him."

Helena wanted to ask what Mari meant, but couldn't find the right words. Edmund seemed to sense the question and mouthed 'later' before crouching in front of Corban. "How many times have I come to you, Corban?"

The boy shrugged.

Edmund smiled fondly. "A lot. You and I are bonded by magic. Mari too. In this city that's very rare. You can trust me. I won't lead you into danger."

Corban nodded. "I trust you."

Edmund smiled and straightened before gripping Corban's shoulder and guiding him to the bed.

Dell murmured something unintelligible as the young boy placed his palms against the unconscious man's chest.

Nothing happened.

Helena looked to Edmund, but he focused on Dell's face.

As she glanced back to Dell, the bruises receded and Helena sucked in a breath. Dell's cut lip stitched itself back together. Helena stumbled back until her butt hit the wall.

Every scratch, every blemish faded away, leaving unmarked bronze skin. Crimson blood still streaked through his jaw length, sun-bleached hair.

He was older than she'd thought him to be during the fight. Dell.

She shook her head vigorously. "This isn't possible."

Mari, who had yet to speak a word to Helena, watched her out of the corner of her eye. The princess pulled her cap down further under the scrutinizing gaze. She knew, didn't she?

Did she know?

Panic clawed at her throat.

Edmund crossed toward her and dropped his voice. "We have a lot to talk about."

"Aw, Edmund." A rich voice called from the bed. "Not going to stay to make sure Corban's mojo is still working?"

Edmund rounded on him. "Five. The number of times I've had to bring you here in the last three months. Do you have a death wish, Dell?"

Dell's vibrant eyes darkened. "Those weren't all my fault and you know it."

"Darn it, Dell." Edmund pulled at the ends of his hair. "If you die…"

Helena didn't know what they were talking about, but curiosity had her moving closer.

"I'm not going to die," Dell said simply.

"The illegal fights. Stealing. Do you even have a head on those shoulders?"

An angry flush rose in the young man's face as if he was about to explode. Helena grabbed Edmund's arm. "Edmund, leave him be."

Dell's anger snapped away in an instant as his eyes fixed on Helena, seeing her for the first time. "Who do we have here?" He sat up to peer closer. "You don't think you're fooling anyone in that getup, do you, miss?"

Helena ripped the hat from her head. Her dark curls spilled out, and she turned to Edmund. "Am I that obvious?"

Edmund bit the inside of his cheek to keep from smiling. "Only to scoundrels and deceivers themselves, my dear." His eyes flicked to each person in the room. "Mari, Corban, I am once again in your debt. I'll pay for this idiot's care. Don't let him return home for a few days. The news of the fight will have spread and we must prevent questions should the king hear."

He turned to Dell with a scowl. "The next time I see you in an illegal boxing match, I'm leaving you in the bloody dirt. Fool. Orlo should have gutted you."

Dell flashed a smile that spoke of no cares. "But then who would you yell at every day?"

Edmund grunted.

"You'd miss this pretty face. Go on, Edmund. Admit it. You care about me."

Edmund's stern facade cracked, and a laugh slipped through. "Okay, Dell. We're leaving."

"Have fun!" He waggled his eyebrows.

They stepped into the front room and Edmund pointed to her hat. "Don't listen to Dell. Put that back on. It's better no one knows you're a woman and puts any of the pieces together."

"Did he think we were—"

"Yep."

She turned. "Shouldn't we tell him that's not—"

"Helena." His stern voice stopped her. "Dell will not speak of anything that happened here. It doesn't matter what he thinks. But you and I need to have a discussion."

As soon as he pulled her onto the street, all sound ceased. A cart passed by, but the wheels made no rumble. Helena turned around to stare wide-eyed at Edmund.

He sighed. "You already know I'm Belaen. Every person with Belaen blood carries magic. Mine is the ability to shift the winds. I'm pushing them away from us. We cannot hear anything. At the same time, I'm pushing a stream of air toward us to trap our own words."

Helena was so lost in her thoughts of magic and the man she thought she'd known, she didn't see the rock in the road. Edmund's hand guided her around it before she fell, bringing her back to their current reality and what she knew was coming.

Edmund's voice was low when he spoke again. "Tell me what you were thinking."

She shrugged. She knew the answer, but he wouldn't understand. How could he?

"Princess."

He only called her princess in formal situations, letting her know he wasn't asking as her friend, but as a member of the royal council.

"Helena," he tried again. "You know the laws."

She did. And she hated them. Tears pricked the corner of her eyes.

"If your father found out, they could take you from the line of succession," he went on. "If the priests found out… Your birthday ball would be canceled."

They both knew the priesthood would do something far worse to her.

To some, the ball seemed silly. Who cared about a

party when freedom was on the line? But that ball was supposed to be where her father made his final decision in who her husband would be.

"I wanted to see my kingdom." The words were small, but she felt every one. She was second in line to the throne. She would one day run the merchant guild.

But she was a princess of Madra, meant to be hidden away like a precious jewel. The law of Madra said few had the privilege to look upon a princess' face until her wedding day. She wasn't allowed outside the palace. When she attended balls and ceremonies, she wore a mask to cover all but her mouth.

It was a terrible law, but a sacred one in the eyes of the priests. The common man's eyes defiled a princess just by gazing upon her. Those were the words of the priesthood.

Edmund only knew her face because his position as ambassador allowed him that privilege.

He rubbed the back of his neck. "I don't know how to do this, Helena. I grew up in Gaule where men like me who prefer men over women were put to death. Here in Madra, we live openly. Yet in Gaule, a woman has every freedom. They are now ruled by a queen. My best friend is the queen of Bela. But we aren't in either of those countries. I want you to have those same freedoms, but I don't want you to lose everything… I don't want to lose you."

He wrapped an arm around her shoulders. "I lost everything once. A king I loved imprisoned me for my deception. I don't want that for you." He squeezed her tighter to his side as they walked. "Please, wear the mask.

Stay in the palace. You've done it for eighteen years. It's only a few weeks until the ball."

She didn't argue, but she made no promises either. She'd finally gotten a taste of freedom and that memory wasn't going anywhere.

They would reveal her face soon enough, but then all of Madra would know her on sight. She had precious little time left to explore her kingdom as one of its loyal subjects.

They reached Edmund's home. "Where'd you leave your horse?" he asked.

"I walked."

He raised a brow. "You just walked out of the palace?"

"When you're going for stealth, you don't steal a horse and thunder out the gates."

He laughed. "Guess not. How'd you get out?"

She pressed her lips together, not wanting to reveal one of Madra's biggest secrets to the Belaen. She trusted Edmund, but…

Did she have a choice?

"The catacombs under the place lead to a network of tunnels throughout the city."

Edmund's eyes widened, and he ran a hand through his hair. "Well, I wasn't expecting that. Secret tunnels under Madra? I thought that was just a myth."

She shrugged. "I don't think my father even knows they exist. Stev and I found them when we were kids."

Edmund laughed. "I'll bet your dad would love to know the heir to the Madran throne grew up playing in the catacombs."

She shrugged, a small smile playing on her lips. "My brothers and I have never exactly played by the rules."

"Do the rest of them know about the tunnels?"

"I showed Kassander once. The others… no."

She glanced toward the ground, wanting this line of questioning to end. Her brothers were not a subject she enjoyed talking about.

Each child born to the royal family had a purpose placed on them the day they first opened their eyes. Stev was to be the next ruler of Madra. Helena would lead the Merchant guild—the most powerful entity behind the king and the priesthood. Kassander was born to be a priest. Quinn and Cole were bastards but in an unusual move, the king recognized them so even they had roles within the kingdom. They were not placed into the line of succession, but were given posts in military command.

Helena turned to Edmund. "Thanks for getting me this far, but I'm okay getting back on my own."

He shook his head. "Stev would kill me if I didn't accompany you."

She narrowed her eyes, realization setting in. "Of course." She walked back toward the street. "Big brother sent you to find me."

"He saw you leave." There was meaning in his words that took her a few moments to understand.

She slowed her steps. "He let me go?"

"He wanted you to have your freedom, even if it meant defying tradition. I've been following you since you reached the columns at the end of the square. I only stepped in when I saw Dell fighting."

"Unbelievable." She shook her head. "Stev is…" Her

brother was always surprising her. He never spoke to her as if he cared, but then he did things like this.

They made it to the far side of the palace where a grate sat above a hole in the ground. It lay hidden beneath a wooden platform. If anyone found it, they'd assume it was only a part of the vast sewer system consisting of shallow clay pipes. An innovation of her grandmother's. Helena bent and lifted the wooden boards to reveal the metal bars. She pulled a rusted key from the string around her neck and bent to turn it in the iron lock. Edmund pulled the bars free.

"Replace this once I'm through," Helena instructed.

Edmund gaped. "I don't like the thought of you going down into that." He stared into the dark.

She shrugged and sat on the edge of the hole, swinging her legs in and dropping onto the ladder.

As she cleared the entrance, Edmund put the iron bars back in place and stared down at her.

"Thanks, Edmund."

He nodded and watched her descend.

The musty smell of the tunnel enveloped Helena as she jumped from the ladder into the ankle-deep water. Kassander's boots would be soaked, but her ten-year-old brother's clothes were the only ones that fit.

Running through the darkened tunnels, she skimmed her hand along the wall to guide her steps. She didn't know how long she walked before a door appeared, light seeping out from underneath.

She bent over, trying to catch her breath. Everything would be okay. Home was right in front of her. Her first ever trip outside the palace hadn't destroyed her life. She glanced back over her shoulder as adrenaline pumped through her. Being out among the people thrilled her. It gave her something she'd been missing most of her life. A sense of connection with the kingdom her family ruled.

She had to get out there again.

As she set her hand on the door, she pushed just as she'd been taught. A soft click sounded and light flooded the tunnel.

She tumbled into the bedroom that had gone unused since their grandmother was alive. The picture slid back into place to conceal the door. She laughed to herself.

A cough interrupted her celebration, and she twisted on her heel to find Stev leaning against the wall with his arms crossed over his chest.

He didn't say a word as he pointed to the table at his side. Her soft mask with ivory lace lay flat against the marble.

She walked forward and picked it up. As she set it against her skin and tied the ribbons at the back of her head, she couldn't help but feel as if the prison Edmund spoke of was now hers.

Satisfied, Stev nodded and left without a word.

It was only then Helena noticed Kassander sitting on the bed, his excitement making his limbs jump.

"Hey buddy," she said. "You can't tell anyone about this, okay?"

"I know. Stev already told me." His bright eyes fixed onto her face. "I like it better when you're not wearing the mask."

She sighed and wrapped both arms around her brother, pulling him into her lap. Resting her chin on his head, she spoke into his soft chestnut curls. "Me too, kid."

Two

Dell's life had never been a fairytale, but there was a time when he didn't dread going home. A time when he'd run through the front door, skid to a halt in front of the table, and steal whatever his mother had spent the day baking.

She'd scold him, but never without a smile on her face. Then she'd ruffle his hair.

Until the day she no longer stood before him. The day they carted him off to live with a father he'd never met and half-brothers he knew nothing about.

He'd been a sad boy with pretty dreams of being welcomed into a family when he'd lost the only one he'd known. But he'd soon learned fantasy only lived to tease you with what you could never have.

His father had been kind, happy to bring Dell into the family. The first few weeks soothed his boyhood mind and made him imagine many years of such contentment. Then his father took ship on a trading mission, hitting the rough seas around the point of Cana in the middle of a storm. He never returned and Dell went from newfound son, to unwelcome houseguest, to stable boy in a matter of a month.

He rolled over on the small cot in Mari and Corban's shop. They'd left it closed for a few days while he was there. It couldn't be said that the son of the great Lady Tenyson was frequenting a healer's shop on the eastern side of the city. If any even knew he belonged to the Tenyson household. His parentage was a well-kept secret in Madra with his family not claiming any connection other than that of master and servant.

The Tenyson's were the current peak of the spiral. Each merchant family in Madra had a rank. Wealth and success affected rank as well as the king's favor and one's position on the council. Dell's father had worked tirelessly to get the family where it was and Dell's step-mother kept them there through nefarious means.

The hierarchy in Madran society was a spiral with each family one step below the prior one. The rise was a struggle, and the fall was great.

The door opened and Mari appeared. She smiled kindly. She'd taken a liking to the man in constant need of Corban's healing.

"How are you feeling, dear?" she asked.

He struggled to sit up, his muscles aching. It was the first time he'd been truly awake since the fight. "You wouldn't happen to have any ale, would you?"

She raised an eyebrow. "Afraid not. Is that what got you into this predicament?"

"No."

She narrowed her eyes in disbelief. He didn't blame her. He was lying after all.

"I've known you since you first arrived in the city." She crossed her arms. "You can't lie to me."

She was right. He'd found comfort in sneaking away to Mari's shop since he was a broken child in need of a friend. He rubbed his hands together, his leather boxing straps still sticky with blood. Not taking his eyes from her, he unwound the leather and released a sigh as cool air touched his bruised knuckles.

"I work hard, Mari." He tried to infuse more age than he had into his voice. "Yesterday morning, I was sent to help unload a shipment at the docks."

She nodded for him to go on.

"I went for a midday bite at the Cooked Goose and who happens by?"

"I can only guess." She twisted around and slammed her palm against the wall. "Catjsa. That woman…" Shaking her head, she turned back to Dell. "You're lucky Orlo didn't kill you for whatever you did with his wife—"

He threw his hands up. "I didn't do anything! I can't help it if she can't keep her hands off me."

Mari advanced. "Dell, you're a sweet boy, but sometimes I think all this fighting has scrambled your brains." She bent down and gripped his chin. "This face, that bloody smile of yours, they're weapons and they will be turned on you time and again."

"Aw, Mari, you trying to tell me you think I'm beautiful?"

She released him and stepped back with a huff. "Do you take anything seriously? You're a Tenyson, Dell." She placed a palm over her heart. "The only one with anything in here since your dear father passed. I don't want you to be taken advantage of by those wanting to start trouble." Mari and Corban knew who he was even though Edmund did not. He couldn't help that. She'd seen the Tenyson crest his brother burned into his foot when he was eleven years old.

He climbed from the bed and stood, his tall frame towering over her. Putting a hand on each of her shoulders, he bent to look her in the eye. "Don't worry about me."

She gripped his wrists and sighed. "I'll always worry as if you were my own son. I'm not the only one either."

He released her and ran a hand through his sweaty hair. "I don't know why Edmund bothers. He's not even Madran. He—"

She interrupted him. "You don't know the kind of things that man has accomplished. If he sees something in you, it's because you're meant for more than scrubbing decks and cleaning stalls."

There'd been a time when he wanted more. A family. A piece of land to farm. His life with his mother had been simple. They lived in the countryside near a small village. They never had much, but it was a good life.

He shook his head to clear it of those thoughts. "I need to wash this grime off my skin. Mind if I head out back."

"Make sure you aren't seen."

He walked from the back room to a separate part of the building where a door led to an alley. The stiff reek of urine hit him as soon as the wind shifted, but he probably smelled just as bad.

He glanced behind him to make sure no one followed and ducked around back behind the row of shops. They were near the docks where boats left to sail up the river and out into the sea. The river narrowed as it bent around to run along the city. A busy street stood between the alley and a row of trees that blocked the water from view.

Dell took a quick glance each way before sprinting between carts ambling along the road and crashing into the tree cover on the other side. The river sparkled where the sun broke through the branches. It flowed slowly as if enjoying the nice day. Large boulders lined the edge of the water and Dell wasted no time stepping onto one and peeling off his shirt before dropping it on the ground. He kicked off his boots and slipped out of his trousers.

Even as a member of one of the wealthiest families in Madra, he kept his dress simple. Okay, it wasn't his choice to make. When he'd first arrived, he'd worn his brothers' old clothing. But with the years of hard labor he'd outgrown them.

A hiss left his lips as he sank into the icy water. His muscles pulled and screamed as he kicked toward the far bank and back again. As soon as his body loosened, he scrubbed the blood and sweat from his skin.

He dipped below the water, the fight still strong in his mind.

Orlo had beaten him. That was a first. In a rematch, Dell could take him down. He was a fighter. He was good. He was strong.

He almost laughed to himself, but he was still under the water.

Who was he kidding? Orlo was a monster of a man.

He looked up and saw a shadow on the far bank. All he could make out through the distortion of water was a pair of trousers. Edmund checking up on him no doubt.

Dell prepared to lunge, a plan forming in his mind. He burst from the water with a roar, water splashing his audience. He twisted to see Edmund's reaction as his feet gained traction on the muddy bottom. The water barely reached his waist now. Rivulets of water streamed down his heaving torso, and his jaw dropped open as he took in the woman who was wringing a cap in her hands.

He froze as she examined her sopping clothes, taking no note of him. When she finally lifted her head, red flooded her cheeks.

She didn't take her eyes away.

Dell, gaining some sense, stepped forward.

"Stop!" she screamed.

He glanced down to see the water no longer covered him. His hands flew down, but he took another step forward.

"I told you to stop right there."

"I don't know you, miss, so I'd take it kindly if you refrained from giving me orders."

"But you… you—"

He climbed from the water completely, no longer bothering to cover himself as he stopped at her side. "I what?"

She turned away abruptly.

He chuckled. "It's okay, miss. I like Edmund. I won't try anything with his…" His eyes scanned her body. "Woman."

The girl hugged her arms across her body.

Dell laughed again as he bent to retrieve his trousers and stepped into them. "Do I make you uncomfortable?"

"Yes." She refused to look at him and amusement warmed Dell against the chilly breeze.

He slid his shirt over his head, shrinking back at the smell. It would have to do.

"Why are you here?" He bent to tie his boots as he waited for her answer. And for that matter, why was she dressed as a boy again? What was Edmund hiding?

She clicked her tongue. "I couldn't stop thinking about that fight the other day." Her voice dropped. "I needed to see if you were okay."

He grinned and looked up at her. "Translation, the Madran girl was curious about the healing Corban did on me and wanted to see if it really worked or if she'd imagined it."

"That's not what I said."

He straightened. "You didn't have to. You've probably never met anyone with magic before that night–Edmund excluded—and the only stories you've heard have come from drunken soldiers who returned from the wars in Bela with tales of magnificent things."

"Even if all that is true," she started stubbornly. "It isn't why I came into the city."

"Ah, so you don't live here." He tapped his nose. "Careful, miss, or I will learn all your secrets."

He turned and walked back toward the road. The girl ran after him. "Where are you going?"

He didn't owe her an explanation, but he found himself in a giving mood. "I can't be seen in this part of the city. Mari will disguise me."

"How?"

He shook his head. "Don't ask questions you won't believe the answers to."

Mari awaited them in her shop, but she wasn't alone. The crown prince of Madra loomed over her, his stern face scanning the room. Two guards stood on either side of the front door.

Estevan Rhodipus turned toward them as they entered, his scowl deepening.

What business did a prince have with Mari?

The raven-haired girl behind Dell ran a hand down her still-wet clothing and sighed. "Stev—your Highness," she mumbled, stumbling into a curtsy.

Dell bowed dutifully, the act clenching something inside him. The Rhodipus line was leading their people into nothing but destruction.

The prince ignored him and fixed his icy eyes on the girl trying to masquerade as a boy. She obviously hadn't fooled many people with her delicate features and sparkling eyes.

"He-" Prince Estevan started before seeming to catch himself. "Hello, Len."

Was that her name?

His eyes bore into hers as if speaking some secret language.

"Yes, your Highness?" She stared right back, defiance in her gaze.

She'd called him 'Stev'. Something didn't add up.

The prince finally turned to Mari. "Len has duties at the palace that she has evaded. She's a… servant there. One of my mother's girls. The queen has asked me to bring her right away."

Right. The queen wouldn't send the prince to fetch a servant.

Dell's eyes flicked between them, his mind putting the pieces together. Edmund hadn't been protecting her for himself. She wasn't his mistress, she belonged to the prince.

If the prince knew how much she'd seen of Dell… her rosy cheeks came back into his mind. It didn't fit. She didn't seem the type to give herself to the prince. Dell barely knew her, but had thought she was more bull-headed than to be led as the prince was leading her now toward the door, his hands like shackles around her wrists.

"Stev," she said so softly it was as if she thought Dell and Mari wouldn't hear. "Please don't tell him. I—"

He released her and turned to face her. She seemed to shrink into herself. "I won't tell him. You will."

Her eyes widened. "No—"

"Come." He took her by the arm roughly.

"No."

"You don't have a choice."

Dell knew he'd regret his next actions, but everything inside him screamed to protect this girl, this Len.

"The lady said she doesn't wish to return with you." He strode forward.

The prince stopped and turned toward him. "This is no business of yours, commoner."

What would his highness think if he knew Dell was a Tenyson? That he'd just insulted the tip of the spiral. If the Tenyson's no longer supported the royal family, Madra would be thrown into civil war.

But he kept his mouth shut. The prince narrowed his eyes, taking in Dell's filthy clothes, the disgust plain on his face.

"I said, Len stays."

The prince barked out a sharp laugh. "Not on your life, boy."

Dell sighed. He hadn't wanted it to come to this. He pulled a knife from a hidden pocket within his cloak.

The prince flicked his eyes from the short blade to Dell's face and a grin stretched his thin lips. "Pulling a weapon on a member of the royal family is punishable by death." He took a step forward. "But I'm not sure that can qualify as a weapon."

Dell felt the tip with his finger. "It has a pointy end."

The prince laughed again and relaxed his stance. "Pointy end? You've obviously spent no time with the army, boy. I could split you open from nose to navel. You a fighter?"

Len chose that moment to be helpful. "He boxes."

The prince raised an eyebrow. "Put that knife away, kid. I'm not going to hurt the girl. She belongs with me, not here—"

"Among your people?"

"Dell," Len warned. "Really. I'm okay."

He didn't even know her. Why didn't he want to let her go? Prince Estevan, for all his faults, didn't have a reputation of debauchery like the bastard princes. He was serious, hard, and had views on the world that would turn Madra to ash, but he wasn't evil. Only misguided.

He spared Dell one more glance before putting his hand on Len's back and ushering her out.

Mari stepped up to Dell's side. Her words held a teasing lilt. "What were you going to do? Fight him with your carving knife? He isn't made of wood."

He studied the knife in his hand. There was little in his life he did for pure enjoyment, but wood carving gave him a sense of peace. He ran his thumb over the family crest on the handle. Not the Tenyson crest. This one belonged to his mother. She'd taught him to create beauty amid the chaos in his life. Amid the pain and the hardship.

He slid the knife back into his shirt pocket and held it against his chest. "I have to go. I've already missed too much work and my step-mother's punishment will only get worse."

Mari clucked her tongue. "Well, you can't be seen in this part of town." She touched his shoulder and warmth flooded him for only a moment before it disappeared.

He'd never get used to her magic. He ran his hands down the front of his shirt. "I don't ever feel as if your magic is working. When I see myself, I don't notice a change."

She smiled. "Because you don't understand how my power works. I don't alter your appearance. I change other's visual perception of you. But it only ever lasts a few hours."

Dell bent to kiss Mari on the cheek. "Thanks, love." He left through the front door, calling back over his shoulder, "I appreciate you!"

Three

Stev barely spoke on the ride through the streets and up the hill where the palace sat nestled among high columns separating it from the surrounding city. There would be no secret tunnels this time. The guards and servant busybodies would have the perfect view of the crown prince dragging a young boy into the palace. Only, she wasn't a young boy.

She was the princess.

But none of them knew her face. Maybe they'd assume it was Kassander who'd run off and the rumors would spread.

She fidgeted in the carriage as the door opened. Stev climbed out and then held a hand up to help her.

She scanned the courtyard for any hint of the priesthood that controlled the lives of Madra's royal family. Her fingers grasped Stev's as if she'd fall apart without him. How was she supposed to face her father after she'd been caught breaking one of the most sacred laws of Madra? It didn't matter that it wasn't fair. That she thought a princess should have as much freedom as any prince.

He would be so disappointed. Her relationship with her father and eldest brother wasn't always smooth, but she didn't want to let them down.

With a sigh, she gripped Stev's hand tighter. "I'm sorry."

His stern face softened, and he ran a hand over the top of her head. "I don't mean to always be so… rough with you, sister. But if something were to happen to you…"

"It won't. No one in the city even knows I'm a girl."

"That boy—"

"Dell? He's harmless… I think. Honestly, I don't really know. He's a bit full of himself. But Edmund knows him. Do you trust Edmund?"

"Of course."

She smiled. Edmund was the one person who could always bring out a lightness in her brother.

"I won't do it again," she said, squeezing his hand.

He scrubbed a hand over his olive-toned face. "Don't make promises you won't keep, Helena. You've seen so little of what's outside these palace walls. But I won't stop coming for you. You're the one person…" He trailed off.

She couldn't remember a time when her brother said so many words to her at once. He wasn't one to talk about his feelings.

She didn't have time to respond because Edmund awaited them amid the stone columns leading up to the steps at the front of the palace.

"Have a fun jaunt?" he asked.

She glared at him. “And just how was it that Stev knew exactly where to find me?”

Edmund fixed her with a disapproving stare.

“I had to know,” she huffed.

“Know what?” Stev asked.

Edmund didn’t take his eyes from Helena. “Is this about the magic or the boy?”

Stev’s eyes widened. “Len knows about Mari and Corban’s magic?”

Helena stumbled away from them. “You know?”

“I am heir to the throne of Madra.”

As if that answer explained anything. The king had many spies throughout the city. Did Stev have some as well?

“Come.” Stev climbed the steps briskly.

Once inside the family quarters of the palace, Helena relaxed. It might have given her freedom to be without the mask, but it still seemed unnatural.

Her maid appeared, a frown etched onto her withered face. Sophia had been with her since birth.

“Child,” the old woman tsked, scanning her clothes up and down.

Edmund and Stev left her without another word and Sophia ushered her toward the washroom. The maid stripped Helena’s clothes from her body without ceremony. As she stepped into the bronze tub and sat in the tepid water, Helena thought of the boy bathing in the river.

His broad chest had shocked her at first and when he’d stepped from the water… She shook her head and focused on his twinkling eyes instead. Under the filth left over from his fight, was a ruggedly handsome man.

A commoner.

What was wrong with her?

In a month's time, she would choose a husband, or at least that was how it would seem. In truth, her father's will meant more than hers. Her life would soon be tied to a very different man. Would he be handsome? Quick to smile? Dell looked as if he was made to laugh. Not like the serious noblemen she'd have to entertain at her ball.

A torrent of water splashing over her head pulled her from her thoughts.

"Sophia," she shrieked.

"Stop daydreaming and scrub. You look more street urchin than princess."

Once she finished and dressed, Sophia pinned her hair up in intricate loops. It took much more time than Helena would have normally liked, but she was grateful for the delay. She knew what her next task would be.

Facing her father.

The walk across blue velvet floors seemed to take forever and no time at all. Dark cherry-wood walls closed in on her like a tunnel until all she could see was the door to the council chambers where her father awaited.

She lifted her hands to her face, feeling around the edges of the mask. Most of the time, it was her prison, but in this moment, the mask calmed her. Not even her father could see what was truly behind it.

The guards nodded as she stopped on the threshold of the open chamber. She ran her hands down the lacy emerald dress Sophia had forced on her. At least the queen would approve.

Helena's eyes scanned the room. A circular table sat in the middle. On the far side, the king bent over a map he'd spread across the surface. A few of his advisors stood near, listening to him speak. Stev and Edmund were among them.

The queen was nowhere to be found, but that wasn't surprising. She preferred not to speak of warfare, and judging by the generals present, that was exactly what was going on. None of the men even noticed her presence.

Behind Stev stood two priests Helena would recognize anywhere. As a girl, they'd taught her the duties of a princess of Madra. Basically, they'd taught her the necessity of hiding her face.

The priesthood in Madra didn't worship a higher power. They spent their lives in contemplation of the past. They wrote laws in their halls before bringing them to the king. They fashioned themselves the protector of Madran tradition, Madran soul. And apparently, revealing the face of a princess before her betrothal would tarnish that soul.

They also controlled the Madran prisons.

Helena had never developed the faith in the priesthood her father had.

"Sire," Edmund's voice snapped her back to the matter at hand. "I really think you can pull your forces from the interior of Bela. Just leave the few stationed at the Draconian border. The others are needed elsewhere."

Where were they needed? Home. The thought came unbidden to her mind. The soldiers were needed at home. Some of them had been away for years. Their wives and children needed them now. The Madran fields and granaries needed them.

She'd never understood her father's constant wars or his acceptance of everything they cost the kingdom.

"No." The king shook his head. "Bela has magic. We must keep our presence there."

"With all due respect, your Majesty." Edmund's voice grew louder. "The Draconian war ended years ago. I know because I was there. I fought alongside your Madran forces and we were grateful for your aid, but your treasury cannot afford to continue keeping an eye on us. You can trust Queen Persinette. Gaule's fear of magic nearly destroyed them, don't make the same mistake."

"We aren't Gaule."

"No," Edmund agreed. "Because it's not too late for you. Your people are suffering because your treasury runs dry, and the men who work the fields are off with the army. You have units in Bela, Gaule, Andes, and Cana."

"We are aiding those kingdoms."

A new voice piped in, one that made her stomach roil. "Maybe you should aid your own kingdom."

Helena's eyes snapped to the speaker.

"Ian," a harsher voice hissed.

The king lifted his eyes. "Young Tenyson, please, tell me what you really think."

Ian opened his mouth again, but an older woman gripped his arm.

"Let me apologize for my son, your Majesty. This is his first meeting of the war council."

The king raised one brow. "We invited you here to observe, boy. Let those with more experience speak."

Ian's jaw clenched, a look Helena had seen before.

He wasn't any younger than Stev, but Stev had been raised for these duties and his voice carried more weight. He also had the good sense to know when not to speak.

Why was Ian invited? His mother, Lady Tenyson, was

not a member of the war council, having no experience in battle. She was a merchant. Yes, the most powerful merchant in Madra, but that wouldn't do much good when speaking of tactics. But Ian had always been favored. It was why she'd had to suffer his company more frequently than she preferred.

He used to pursue her openly, but that all changed when she embarrassed him in front of her brothers by refusing to spend time alone with him. She'd admit, she was harsh, and it hadn't helped that her brothers started laughing. Since then, he'd treated her with nothing but scorn.

Hands slid around Helena's waist from behind and she squealed as her feet left the ground.

"Hiya, sister." Cole laughed.

She turned when he put her down and threw her arms around him. "Cole, you're back!"

An identical copy of Cole entered behind him. "Quinn!"

The bastard princes had left more than a year ago with a unit of the army sent to drive off a Madran mercenary force in Cana.

She released Cole and threw herself at Quinn.

He squeezed her tightly. "Missed you, sis."

She'd missed them. Cole and Quinn's absence had been wholly felt.

The entire room had quieted and turned to them.

"What are you doing here?" she asked Quinn.

"We wouldn't miss your ball." Cole smirked before walking to shake Lady Tenyson's hand and give Ian a hug. Cole was almost closer to their family than his own.

Quinn crossed to his father and offered his hand.

"Welcome home, son," the king said.

Quinn then gave Stev a hug and shook a few more hands.

Helena took a tentative step into the room. She caught Stev's eye. He frowned and studied her for a moment before shaking his head. Relief shot through her, and she lifted her chin. Stev had decided not to tell their father of her trip into the city.

Quinn stepped back to her side and leaned in. "What did you do?"

"I don't know what you're talking about," she responded.

"I've been here two seconds and can already see the warning looks Edmund is shooting toward Stev. In turn, Stev is glaring at you."

I gave Stev a grateful smile as I leaned closer to Quinn. "He's saving me."

The king finally noticed her presence. "Helena, I'm sure you have better things to do."

She sighed. As a girl, she'd spent countless hours sitting in on war meetings, fascinated. As she grew older, it wasn't considered proper. She was second born, meaning her only worry need be the council of merchants she'd one day lead.

As she turned to leave, she felt a set of eyes following her and her gaze met Ian's. A shiver raced down her spine because everything suddenly made sense. Why he was there.

The Madran law stated a princess would choose her own husband as long as he was of Madran descent. That was the reason for the ball—but her father was known to always weight his dice.

Wouldn't it be a great feat to tie the royal family to the highest of the merchants? The throne would have a power that hadn't been seen in a long time.

She made it back to the royal residence and ripped the mask from her face.

She wouldn't do it. The Tenyson's were vile, conniving, wretches. She'd seen the lecherous looks both sons sent her way.

Her father could make deals all he wanted, but there was one thing she knew for certain.

She would never marry a Tenyson.

Four

An icy blast of water struck Dell's face, and he sputtered awake, almost falling from his loft in the barn. His eyes snapped open to find the haggard face of his stepmother hovering over him. She threw the now empty wooden bucket behind her and planted both hands on her expensive gown covered hips.

He would have laughed at her presence among the un-mucked stalls and animal smells, but her shrill voice permeated the air instead.

"You ungrateful boy. Where have you been? No one has seen you in days."

He may have thought she'd worried over his absence if he didn't know her.

He would not tell her the truth, so he decided to go with nothing at all.

She narrowed her eyes. "You will make up the work. The Madran trader, our largest ship, is leaving a day late to pick up the next shipment coming across the border into Bela. It leaves on the noon tide. Get to the ship."

The Madran Trader has been his father's prized ship. He shook his head. His father was dead. None of the ships were his anymore. They belonged to the Tenyson trading company. An operation he should have been more involved in than cleaning decks.

His stepmother turned and stomped across the straw-covered floor before flinging open the wooden door.

Dell groaned as he sat up and flipped wet hair out of his eyes. A few of the stable lads were waking in their beds. When Dell had first arrived at Tenyson manor and the storm took his father, he couldn't understand why the rest of his supposed family would force him to live with the help. Over the years, he'd been glad of it. It was better than suffocating inside that house.

He climbed from the bunk and slid his shirt off, finding a dry one to replace it. Corban's healing was incredible and efficient, but it used the body's own energy to heal and he felt it for days in the strain of his muscles.

He rubbed his eyes and flattened his hair. Time for another day of working for people who could destroy him if he refused. He had no other choices. No money. No family other than the Tenysons.

Nothing.

He'd made peace with this life a long time ago. His only other option was to join one of the mercenary troops and he wasn't prepared for that.

The sun had yet to appear when he left the barn behind. A few shop owners were preparing for the day. The smell of fresh baked bread hung in the air. Dell glanced back over his shoulder to make sure his stepmother hadn't followed him before ducking inside the bakery.

Agathe, the bakery owner stood at the counter shaping unbaked loaves. "Dell." She smiled. "It's been a few days, honey."

"Morning." He walked forward and kissed the old woman's cheek. Her hair was pulled back from her face in a neat bun, revealing intelligent eyes. He leaned against the counter. "I was with Mari and Corban."

"Uh oh." She grinned. She'd always taken great entertainment in his antics. "Who did you fight this time?"

"Orlo."

She choked on a breath. "We need to work on that brain of yours, boy." She laughed. "Or maybe it's the ego that needs work."

He shrugged and snagged a pastry from the bin. She slapped his hand.

He reached into his pocket and procured one of the few silver coins he had left.

"Do I want to know how you got that?" Agathe asked.

"Probably not."

She lifted a flour-covered hand and patted his cheek. "I'm not taking your money, boy. Just come back this evening. You can eat dinner with me and share more of those joyful smiles." She wiped her hands on her apron. "I swear, you keep me young."

He kissed her cheek again. "You've got yourself a date."

He shoved the rest of the pastry into his mouth as he stepped back out onto the street.

The city spread out before him as the sun peeked

over the two story wooden shops. Flat, terracotta roofs spanned the horizon.

A horse's hooves echoed against the stone road. Dell loved Madra. Since arriving in the city, they'd welcomed him with open arms. Shopkeepers had kept an eye on the wild boy who never seemed like he had enough to eat.

They'd given him their children's old clothing.

He was one of them.

Only, he wasn't.

Because Dell was a merchant's son. His family's ships brought the goods sold in their shops and they used their power to control their daily lives. The Tenyson boys bullied the common kids through their adolescence and continued to lord their control even into adulthood.

What would people like Agathe think if they knew Dell carried the Tenyson name as well?

He smiled at the portly fellow opening the butcher shop, trying to hide the confusion swirling in his mind. He wanted to belong among them.

A breeze whipped through the streets, carrying the odor that told of a proximity to the sea. They called Madra the gateway kingdom. Goods passed through between Bela and Gaule and the Kingdoms to the North. The docks were their point of entry and an impressive one at that.

Outside the city, one could find spots to gaze out at the sea, but the docks themselves sat in the widest part of the river.

Long wooden piers stretched as far as he could see to the left and right. Some were empty, but most housed merchant vessels, their sails flapping in the wind like the beat of a familiar drum. A few war vessels were in, but most had carried their troops to the various fronts ordered by the king.

Sailors called greetings to Dell. In their eyes, he was no different from them. They worked their fingers to the bone every day with no chance for respite.

Dell's feet took him to a row of ships belonging to the Tenyson family. Grant, his stepmother's most favored captain, spotted him and jumped his thick frame from the rigging, landing on the deck with a defining thud.

"You're late." He scowled.

Dell wasn't late, but Grant said it every time.

Grant walked toward the rail where a mop leaned next to a bucket of muddy brown water. "Galley needs cleaned." He walked away.

Stretching his neck from side to side, Dell reached for the bucket. He wrapped his fingers around the mop and kicked open the door before descending into the darkness.

Dell worked tirelessly until dark—Grant didn't allow breaks—and when he finally decided it was quitting time, Dell found his brothers waiting for him at the side of the ship.

Setting his hands on the rail, he leaped over, stumbling from exhaustion as he landed.

Ian let out a low chuckle and stepped forward. Reed hung back. It was how it always was with them. Ian led and Reed followed.

"Where have you been?" Ian asked.

Dell brushed a hand through his sweat-soaked hair. "Right here."

Ian shoved him back. "Before today. You've been missing."

"Aw." Dell leaned close, a smirk planted on his lips. "I'm touched you care."

He saw the punch coming even before Ian lurched forward, so he ducked out of the way. Ian lunged again, but Dell was quick. All the time he spent boxing paid off. He shifted his feet and the next time Ian's arm shot out, he grabbed his wrist and twisted it down before delivering a blow to his brother's cheek.

"Reed," Ian growled.

Like a dog responding to its master, Reed advanced. Dell glanced between them. Each was larger than him and with his fighting skills he could take down one. But what then? What would his stepmother do?

So, he did the only thing he could think of.

Dell ran, his exhausted legs stumbling the first few steps.

He wasn't proud of it, but he had no choice. If they'd been anyone else, he'd have taken them on and fought until he couldn't anymore. But his brothers were untouchable.

He made it to the end of the docks and heard their steps thundering after him, punctuated by Ian's yelled threats. He turned onto the street and ducked into an alley, jumping over something he barely even saw without breaking his speed.

He hurtled onto the next street and was halfway down when someone yelled to him sharply.

"Dell."

Dell's feet skidded to a halt, and he turned to find Edmund standing with Agathe in front of her bakery.

Edmund walked into the street just as Ian and Reed appeared. They stopped a few yards away, their eyes seething. They didn't dare touch Dell with the Belaen Ambassador present.

Dell bent over, gasping for breath as the day's work caught up with him.

How was Edmund always so calm?

Edmund straightened his shoulders to face Dell's brothers.

Agathe stepped up beside Dell. "It's okay, dear."

Dell's mind spun rapidly. "You know who I am? Does everyone?" He glanced toward the row of deserted shops.

"Only me," she assured him. "And only for the last few months."

Edmund's voice was not one to argue with. "You Tenyson's…" He shook his head. "I have only been in Madra a year, but even I know how the tip of the spiral is supposed to behave. Mistreating your brother is below your station."

"He's not our brother," Ian growled. "Just a servant."

A blast of air whipped around them, trapping them as it swirled. Edmund's voice seemed to carry on the wind itself.

"You will leave Dell to attend his duties in peace. The next person to lay a hand on him will answer to me."

The wind dropped and silence descended on them until they could hear again. "Do you understand?" Edmund's voice lowered again.

Ian and Reed didn't respond. Instead, they turned and walked away as fast as they could without it seeming like they were running.

Dell grinned at Edmund and started a slow clap. "Bravo, friend. You just made the sons of the most powerful merchant in Madra wet themselves."

Agathe shook her head. "You're a vulgar one, Dell." She eyed Edmund. "If you're okay, I still have to lock up for the night."

Edmund nodded. "I must speak to Dell."

"We'll reschedule our dinner, Dell." Agathe left, and Dell stared at the ground, kicking a rock with his toe. He was losing count of how many times Edmund showed up to help him, but his gratitude was lost in a desire to get home and collapse into his loft.

Edmund stood still for a moment, glancing toward the far end of the street. A half-moon hung overhead, giving them what little light it had.

Dell finally lifted his eyes. "You've got to give me something, sir. Why are you here?"

Edmund didn't have to ask what he meant. The question wasn't why was he in Madra, but why did he continue to come to Dell's aid.

Edmund studied him. "I had a hard time for many years." He walked toward one of the shops and sat on the ground to lean against the wall. Dell followed him, lowering himself to the ground with a relieved sigh.

"My father was—is—an angry man," he continued.

"We have that in common. My stepmother…" Dell rested his arms on his knees.

"We do, but I'll bet your stepmother never wanted you dead."

Dell snapped his eyes to Edmund's. "She may wish it, but she'd never do it. However vile that woman is, she loved my father."

"It was the magic. For a long time, the people of Gaule hated those of us with it. It made me an angry kid.

I had to hide this huge part of myself. But that wasn't the worst of it. I had no family. I was alone."

Dell watched him with rapt attention. "What changed?"

"Loyalty. I met the prince of Gaule. He didn't ask for my loyalty, only my friendship, but that loyalty saved me. My life had purpose. I would protect the future reign of Alexandre Durand."

"I thought he was the king of Bela?" Dell asked.

Edmund laughed. "It's a long story. But yes, he rules alongside Queen Persinette and she now has my loyalty as much as Alex."

"This is interesting and all, but I don't see what it has to do with me."

"Dell." Edmund searched Dell's eyes and when he seemed to find what he was looking for, he spoke again. "Give me your loyalty."

Dell startled. "Edmund, I appreciate everything you've done for me, but… isn't that treason? To pledge myself to someone not of Madran blood?"

"Yes. You will break laws. You could end up dead. But Dell, you could also finally find something worth fighting for."

Flashes of Dell's street fights rolled through his mind in quick succession. Women. Debts. Sometimes no reason at all.

What would it be like to fight for something real?

What did he really know about Edmund? Not much. Everything inside him screamed that Edmund was someone to trust. Dell so desperately wanted one person, anyone to have faith in.

But something didn't add up.

"What's going on, Edmund? You're asking me to trust you, so you need to trust me as well. Why do you need me? You work for the royal family. They have people at their beck and call. Or you could have some loyal Belaen take ship."

Edmund leaned his head back against the wall. "You're right." He paused. "But I need someone who knows the streets of Madra. There is going to be a coup. They will overthrow the king."

Five

Helena's mother was not of Madran blood. As heir to the throne, her father had to marry a foreign woman of high importance. Cana didn't have princesses or kings. The clans were not unified in their kingdom.

Queen Chloe was the daughter of a powerful Canan warlord who had kept other clans in check for many years.

But that wasn't all she was. They had trained Chloe Rhodipus to be an assassin. It was the way of Cana. All highborn lads and ladies held skills in the art. Cana was a nest of snakes. None of the clans trusted any other. Being clan-leader was a dangerous position.

Helena flipped a knife in her hand, eying her target. Most in Madra—including the king himself—did not know of the queen's talents. But she'd followed the traditions of her kingdom and brought her daughter up to know what it was to fight.

A cracked wooden post sat forty paces from Helena in

the empty space. She practiced in a little-used training yard, hidden from the main training ground by a high partition. Her mother's guards stood at the door, making sure unwelcome intruders would not find the princess there.

Helena bent her knees and tilted her shoulder down before lifting her arm and flicking her wrist to send the knife end over end. It collided with the wood, a soft thud reaching her ears. The corner of her mouth ticked up. Not even her brothers knew of the talents she'd practiced for years.

She considered seeking her mother to show her the improvements she'd made in the techniques she was learning, but today was not the day for that. A foreign princess would soon arrive at their shores. The queen would set out to meet her soon.

Helena sighed as she walked forward and bent to retrieve the knife.

One of the guards stepped up, and she handed the weapon to him. "Thanks, Kolettis."

He dipped his head. "You're improving, Princess."

Pride bloomed within her at the recognition. Her brothers always proved their worthiness but as the hidden princess, she had little chance to be anything other than a mystery to most people.

"My mother is a good teacher," she responded. "I'm going to find my brothers. You can return to my mother."

"As you wish."

She resisted the urge to sigh again. The formality always grated on her. It was as if the people of the palace feared her. In truth, they just didn't know her. Not like they did her brothers.

She passed under the narrow stone archways that led to the main training yard, and the clash of swords caused her to stop.

Helena watched the twins in fascination. They moved parallel to each other, perfectly in sync as they battled. When Quinn jabbed to the right, Cole knew it was coming. When Cole twisted and tried to take out Quinn's leg, his twin saw it before it happened.

She'd always been jealous of their bond. The bastard princes hadn't grown up with the privilege she enjoyed along with Stev and Kass. They enjoyed more freedom.

The twins were raised in a tavern until they were ten years old and their mother died. It was only then the king admitted to the knowledge of their existence. It wasn't unusual in Madra for the king to sire many children. In fact, it was expected. That was how a royal family cemented their power—by spreading it out among different parts of the kingdom. The monarchy. The council of merchants. The priesthood. The army. Recognizing Quinn and Cole as royals expanded the Rhodipus' control. It left only one faction without a royal—the priesthood. But Kassander would one day fill that role.

Even after they were taken into the palace, Quinn and Cole were united against the world. But never against Helena.

Kass bumped Helena's elbow. "Will I fight like them some day?"

She smiled, her cheeks pressing against the soft mask. Many days, she stayed hidden in the family residence to avoid wearing the thing. She looked to the sky, longing to feel the sun warm her face.

"You're to be a priest, Kass. You'll fight with your words." She ruffled his hair.

"And you, Len? What will you fight with?"

The question was one she'd asked herself many times. As head of the council, she wasn't sure what she'd be fighting for. When she saw her future, she wanted to be anyone but the princess of Madra.

"I'll… I guess I'll use my intellect to fight." Not her knives as she preferred.

Kassander scoffed. "Sounds boring."

She laughed, the sound loud enough to reach the twins who both stopped fighting to turn to her. "It does. Doesn't it?"

Kassander shrugged.

Cole ran toward them, his bare chest glistening with sweat. "Didn't know we had an audience."

"I didn't get much of a chance to speak with you yesterday." Helena shot her brother a grin.

Quinn stepped up beside Cole. Every inch of them was identical, but she'd been able to tell them apart from the first day they arrived eleven years before. Cole had an infectious joy, an incredible zeal for life. But he'd never opened himself up to the family. The hatred between him and Stev was too much to bear at times and occasionally she caught him eying their father with the same dislike. But he loved her and Kassander.

Quinn had become a part of them. No one was as close to him as Cole, but he'd still crafted strong bonds with everyone else. He had a calm confidence about him that was unmistakable.

"Hey Kassander." Cole grinned. "Take Quinn's sword."

Kassander looked to her as if asking permission. She nodded, and he followed Cole across the training yard.

Quinn crossed his arms over his chest and watched as Cole let Kassander chase him with the sword before turning on him to teach him a few moves.

"I missed you two," Helena said.

"I heard what you've been up to." Unlike with Stev, there was no disappointment in Quinn's voice, only curiosity.

"Edmund or Stev?" she asked in resignation.

"Our brother is only worried. Should he be?"

"I'm being careful. Quinn, there's so much to see. The city. The people."

"If you're amazed by Madra, you should see Cana." That was why she loved Quinn. He wouldn't judge her for her deceptions or stress over her. He could move on. "Mother Chloe was right. It's a beautiful country. Dangerous too."

"Are you going back?"

He shook his head. "After your ball, I am being sent to Gaule with my troops. We're the aid promised in the betrothal agreement between Stev and the princess Camille."

"Have you met her?" They'd all been told of Camille Durand, the widowed princess of Gaule. Her husband caught an illness more than a year before and died in his bed.

"I've heard stories, but most people only speak of her brother and his queen."

"The king of Bela?" She shivered. "Is Queen Persinette really as powerful as the stories? Her magic…"

"They say it's mostly gone."

Disappointment seeped into her. Thinking of an all-powerful queen had led to many fantasies.

Quinn glanced toward Cole again. "He is to stay though." He put a hand on her shoulder. "Once you're betrothed, you will gain your own guards. Cole is to choose them."

She nodded, thankful for that. Once she could go into the city as the princess rather than disguised as a boy, guards would accompany her, and if her brother chose them, she knew she'd be safe.

Cole and Kassander dropped their swords and wrestled in the dirt, their laughs punctuated by grunts.

Footsteps echoed along the corridor leading to the training yard seconds before the queen appeared. Helena's mother smiled when she saw her children. Every bit of hardness in their father was countered with love from their mother.

Her long purple gown swept along the ground, giving her the appearance she was floating. She looked every bit the regal queen, but Helena knew where each knife was hidden among the folds of her dress.

"Quinn." The queen stopped in front of him and touched his cheek. "It's good to have you home."

The twins might not be hers, but the queen tried to be a mother to them.

"I'm glad to be here." Quinn smiled back at her.

Cole got to his feet and lifted Kassander onto his shoulders. The boy shrieked as they trotted toward the queen.

"Mother." Kassander giggled as Cole slid him down.

"Looks like someone is having a good time." She

turned her eyes on Cole, the same sadness in them as every other time she looked at him.

"Your Majesty." Cole's joy seeped out of him.

He'd never accepted Chloe Rhodipus as his mother. Helena wondered if it was out of loyalty to his long-dead mother or something else.

Quinn put a hand on Cole's shoulder. "Come, brother. We should go see father about our duties preparing for the ball." He gave the queen an apologetic smile and led his twin away.

The queen's shoulders only dropped for a moment before she pasted on a cheery smile and turned to her other two children.

"Come. You two must prepare. We're to greet a ship from Gaule."

Helena froze. "I am to go?" They had never allowed her into the city even wearing her masks. She longed to see the ships that fed the kingdom's economy but had yet to make it that far in her disguise.

Her mother put a hand on her back to lead her forward. "The people must see you before the ball and this is the perfect chance."

"Who is coming on that ship?"

She smiled slyly. "Your brother's betrothed."

Helena nearly choked. How could the Gaulean princess be arriving and the palace not be abuzz? Where were the preparations? Feasts?

As if reading her mind, the queen explained. "The princess made certain demands of us. No public spectacles. We may greet her at the ship but then must whisk her to the privacy of the palace. She's only here for a short time and we don't want word getting out. She made the crossing because she demanded to meet your brother before agreeing to marry him."

"Will she be staying until the ball?"

"Yes, dear. That's the plan. We're announcing the betrothal at your ball."

They followed their mother back into the palace where Sophia was waiting with a special kind of torture for Helena. A corseted dress.

Helena sighed as her maid led her into her room and helped her dress. As Sophia pulled the corset ties tight, Helena reminded herself if it meant venturing into the city, she'd wear anything.

That thought broke away as she tied her mask to her face. This wouldn't be like before. This trip wasn't about freedom. It was the opposite. She was showing the people that their royal family adhered to the ancient laws.

A carriage waited at the bottom of the palace steps. Her mother and Kassander were already seated inside. She ran a hand over the soft white coat of one of the horses before climbing inside and shutting the door. A host of guards on horseback formed up around them and they thundered through the gates and onto the road that led to the docks.

The guards cleared the street in front of them so the carriage could pass easily between the buildings that were packed together. A crowd formed to watch them go by.

"I wish I could go on a ship," Kassander said.

The queen smiled at her son. "Maybe one day we'll go see the rolling hills of Bela."

Helena stayed quiet as she glanced out the window. They all knew they'd never be allowed to venture outside Madra. Maybe Kassander would as a member of the clergy. But the king always said the world wasn't a safe place. The queen and princess would stay within the Madran borders.

"Mother," Helena began. "Why was I allowed to come today?"

Sadness flickered across the queen's face. "We are welcoming a foreign princess. You will help her adjust to Madra." She paused, but Helena could tell she wasn't finished. "I know the mask hasn't been easy for you and I wish I could take away all the suffering it has caused. But we must obey your father and he must follow tradition."

The corner of her mouth curved up. "But I won't tell him about your trips into the city."

Helena's jaw dropped open. "How—" Her eyes found Kassander, and she laughed. "Of course."

Her mother's face grew serious. "But Len, you must not go again. It's dangerous to disobey the priesthood. I don't worry about you without your guards because you can take care of yourself. I worry about what will happen if others find out you've revealed your face."

"No one even knows it's me."

"And if they found out? Promise me you're finished and I'll keep it to myself."

Helena sighed, fingering the knife she kept in a hidden pocket of her dress. "Fine."

The carriage came to a stop and Helena waited for someone to open the door. As soon as it swung wide, she sucked in a breath.

The docks.

Ships of every size bobbed in the sparkling water. Colorful sails billowed out as the stiff breeze caught them.

Sailors climbed ropes, scrubbed decks, and shouted to each other.

A hand appeared to help her out, and she took it, coming face to face with Edmund.

"Princess." He grinned. "What a lovely day for a jaunt."

"Ambassador." The queen took his hand next. "I hope you haven't been waiting long?"

"No, your Majesty." He turned back to the carriage and lifted Kassander out. "The ship has just arrived."

"Let's not waste any time now. I'd like to meet this delightful princess who will be a new daughter."

Edmund bit his lip to contain a laugh. As the queen and their guards walked across the wooden planks of the docks, Helena grabbed Edmund's arm. "What's so funny?"

"I've just never heard anyone call Camille delightful before."

"Is she that bad?"

"She used to be."

They came to an abrupt halt near a long wooden pier jutting out toward a ship that rose with the timing of the waves. The ship collided with the peer and a loud crack rent the air. Helena jumped.

Edmund glanced at her out of the corner of his eyes, an amused grin on his face.

The crowds behind them buzzed with energy but none were allowed near the royals or this mysterious new visitor. Three priests stood to the back of the crowd watching. Always watching.

The guards moved aside to let two dockworkers run

toward the ship as someone threw ropes over the sides with shouts of greeting.

Blonde hair gleamed in the sun as one of the men heaved on the ropes, and Helena recognized him instantly.

Dell.

He moved with confidence in everything he did. It was fascinating. Why was she so interested in him?

Dell flicked hair out of his bronzed face and flashed a smile at the other man with him. The second man narrowed his eyes and barked out a harsh "Get moving."

As he ran the length of the ship, Dell's lean muscles flexed. Beneath her mask, Helena was sure her cheeks were aflame.

She'd seen those muscles. All of them.

So, he was a sailor? This boy who fought in the middle of the street? Who bathed in the river? He was a riddle, and she wanted nothing more than to figure him out.

Helena had never had a friend before—not that Dell could count as that. But he'd risked himself trying to save her from Stev. He didn't know there was no need to defend her.

Sure, she'd been surrounded by her brothers her entire life. And she loved them. But there was a distinct difference between the ones always trying to keep you safe and the ones who gave you a reason to take risks.

Which one was Dell?

He lifted a long plank of wood and used it to connect the ship to the dock for those aboard to step across. Once the board was stable, he glanced over his shoulder as if seeing the queen, prince, and princess for the first time.

Saying something to the other man that made him scowl, Dell walked their way.

Helena held her breath, reminding herself there was no way he could recognize her in a corseted dress and mask.

"Your Majesty." He bowed to the queen.

Helena's mother shook off her surprise at his approach. None of the other sailors dared accompany him.

"Hello, young man." The queen gestured for him to straighten. "Thank you for your assistance today."

Dell shrugged. "It's my job."

A few people nearby gasped at his words and their informality. This was why the royal family rarely associated with the common people. That was what Stev would have said. Commoners didn't understand how to behave with grace.

But Helena wasn't Stev. A laugh escaped her lips, and she slapped a hand over her mouth, shocked at herself.

Dell flashed her his dimples before reaching out to ruffle Kassander's hair, turning on his heel without being dismissed, and returning to the side of the ship.

Edmund put a hand over his face. "That boy…"

Helena's mother opened her mouth to say something and then shut it again. She shook her head. "I don't know, Ambassador. I rather liked him."

"Me too, mother." Helena refused to meet Edmund's eyes, but she could feel him watching her.

Finally, a horn sounded. A moment later, guards in the forest green uniforms of Gaule marched from the ship.

Next came the maid. There was only one of them,

which shocked Helena. When Stev traveled, he took an entire host of servants with him as if he couldn't wipe his own bum without assistance.

As soon as Princess Camille appeared, Helena knew it was her. She carried herself as someone who'd been born into an important position.

Dark hair curled around a heart-shaped face. Keen eyes scanned the waiting party. Her slender frame was almost hidden among her much larger guards. She was younger than Helena expected. This was the widowed princess?

The guards parted and Kassander gaped beside Helena. Helena herself was quicker to hide any reaction. Camille limped forward, one foot dragging. She leaned her weight on a four-pronged cane before moving it forward. It clacked against the wood beneath it.

"Mother," Helena whispered. "Did you know?"

"We know everything, Helena."

Edmund rushed forward and pushed through the guards to help Camille. She didn't smile when she saw him, but Helena would have sworn her shoulders sagged in relief. He wrapped his arms around her for a moment before releasing her and extending an arm for her to take.

They made their way over slowly. Camille dipped into a curtsy and Helena couldn't take her eyes from the cane.

But the queen was better at concealing her curiosities than her daughter. "Princess, we are honored to have you with us."

"Gaule is honored by this alliance."

Nothing about herself, only her kingdom.

Kassander recovered from his initial shock. He bowed to Camille. "My lady."

Amusement lit in Edmund's eyes, but it turned to concern as he took in Camille's blank expression.

"Can we leave now?" she asked.

"Yes, dear." The queen signaled one of the guards.

Edmund rode in the carriage with them back to the palace, not wanting to let Camille out of his sight as they left the city outside the gates.

Six

Helena had dreamed of having a sister. What would it be like? Would she be more friend than protector?

But she lived her life surrounded by boys who excluded her. They eventually turned into men who protected her at the expense of her even having a chance at a life beyond the palace.

None of her brothers had married yet. They were all of age except for Kassander, but in Madra, royal marriages had to occur in the order of the succession line.

They'd searched for someone worthy of Stev. The heir to the throne had a duty to make a strong alliance with his marriage.

What did the king fear more than anything? The kingdoms full of magic. That made Gaule a natural ally. Even a widowed princess with a twisted foot would do if it gave Madra a stronger foothold across the sea and an ally who feared magic as much as them.

Helena stared at Camille across the sitting room. The Gaulean princess sipped her tea, acting as if no one else was even in the room. Stev sat nearby, his fists clenching in agitation.

Camille had been there for two days and barely spoken to anyone but Edmund or her own guards.

Stev stood abruptly and stormed from the room. Camille let out an audible breath.

Helena couldn't take it anymore. "I know nothing about you."

Camille lifted her eyes. "What?"

"We have stories here in Madra about Gaule and Bela. Queen Persinette, King Alexandre, Queen Catrine, Prince Tyson, but not you. I've never heard of Princess Camille."

She ran her hands through her hair before twisting it over one shoulder. "I…" She stopped.

"I didn't mean you have to tell me." Helena crossed her arms. "I don't really care. All I'm saying is that you sit here in our home and act like Madra is so completely beneath you, and yet, you aren't even mentioned by the minstrels when they talk of Bela and Gaule winning the war against Dracon. How important could you really be?"

Tears formed in Camille's eyes and Helena instantly regretted her brash words.

"I'm sorry," Camille whispered. "I just don't know how…" She wiped her eyes. "I don't know how to do this again."

"Do what?"

"Marry a man I don't know. My kingdom needs this alliance. My mother's wish is to create a world where each kingdom is tied to the others to prevent the kind of war that happened before. I'm her tie to Madra."

"You're the kingdom's tool."

Camille nodded. "Again. This is the second time I've had to marry for the good of the kingdom."

Helena stood and crossed the room before dropping onto the couch beside Camille. "I know how you feel. I get to choose my husband as long as he's Madran… that's the official law… but my father will be the real decision maker at the ball."

"We hear stories in Gaule as well." Camille's eyes scanned the mask covering Helena's face. "Of the hidden princess. Must you always shield your face? That's a terrible burden."

She had no idea, Helena thought. She closed her eyes and breathed in deep. Not a burden, a duty.

Before Helena could utter another word, Edmund appeared in the doorway. "Princesses."

"Edmund." Helena raised a brow at his hesitancy.

"Stev has asked me to take Camille into the city. He'd like her to see more of Madra than this palace."

More than anyone had ever wanted for her, Helena thought. Edmund's eyes bore into her. How could he always read her thoughts?

"Just go," she snapped.

When they were gone, she pulled her feet up under her and untied the laces of her mask. It fell to the ground as if it held all the weight of the world.

Maybe not the world, but every bit of weight she carried with her rested in the curves of that fabric.

Seven

"Be loyal to me, Dell," Dell grumbled as he jammed the shovel into another pile of horse crap. "I'll give you something to fight for." He dumped the manure in the bucket and went for another. "Load of bollocks."

The horse in the neighboring stall kicked at the wall separating them and Dell shook his head. "Relax, Ian." He'd named the horse after his eldest brother. Maybe it was the long, ugly face or the arrogant disposition that reminded him of his brother.

Each of his family members had a namesake in the barn. Reed was the pig in the end stall that failed to thrive on his own.

And Dell's stepmother? Well, she was the single cow they owned.

These weren't their actual names, of course, but it gave Dell some small pleasure.

He leaned his shovel against the wall, his mind going to Edmund once more. He'd told him the king would be overthrown, and then he left.

Dell wasn't even sure which side he was on.

Because the only thing he was sure of, was that Edmund had his loyalty before even asking for it. He wasn't even Madran, but he looked out for Dell.

Dell had few people who cared if he survived each night. He had to hold on to the ones who were there.

But, what the hell? Edmund couldn't just tell him Madra would change forever and not give him any details.

Did Dell want the king overthrown? He knew what most of the common people thought. King Rhodipus' wars drained the kingdom of everything. Man-power… food. Most had family members off with the army or the mercenaries. Sometimes it was the only way to keep a family fed.

Unless you were the bastard son of a dead merchant who left his family with wealth and power. Then the way to keep fed was cleaning decks and shoveling dung.

Dell wiped his sweaty face on his tunic as he watched Ian continue to kick the stall door.

"You aren't getting out, you bastard." He reached into a bag hanging on the stall and procured an apple. Ian snapped at it, and Dell pulled it back. "Someone's in a bad mood. Now Ian, do I have to teach you some manners?"

He grinned at the thought of his brother having manners of any kind. At least there was still hope for horse-Ian.

"Get your brains scrambled in another fight, lad?" Edmund chuckled from the doorway.

Dell tossed the apple to Ian. The horse caught it in his mouth, and it crunched as he ate it whole.

Dell turned. "Why Edmund, what a nice surprise. I didn't know you remembered little old me."

Edmund crossed his arms and didn't respond.

Dell scanned the woman holding the ambassador's arm. She wore a hood, concealing her face in shadow, but as she stepped forward, Edmund moved in sync with her as if holding her up, and it gave away her identity.

"Princess." Dell swept his arm out in an elaborate bow. "Who did you piss off at the palace to get stuck with Edmund for company?"

A muffled laugh came out of the small woman. "I like this boy, Edmund. Can I take him back to Gaule with me?"

"Sorry, Princess. His stepmother might miss the free labor." Edmund threw the words out as if they were a joke, but Dell winced. It was true. His family wouldn't allow him to leave because he served them, not because they cared for him.

Princess Camille pushed back her hood, revealing long raven hair and piercing blue eyes. "Your mother owns this manor?" She threw a look at the great house behind her, its columned splendor rising above the squalor of the city at its gates. The Tenyson's lived outside the merchant sector. Lord Tenyson's grandfather hadn't trusted the scheming of merchant families desperate to climb to the top of the spiral.

Camille's tone held no accusation or suspicion, only curiosity, but he didn't want to speak of family history with a near stranger.

Dell shrugged. "Stepmother."

Edmund seemed to sense his discomfort. "Dell, I need to speak with you."

"I have work to do. Not all of us can befriend a king, get sent as an ambassador who never seems to have to do anything, and then sit on his ass." He turned to grab the shovel again.

Edmund waited a moment as Dell got back to work. "Noon. Come to the back gate of my home. One of my men will let you in. We will be waiting."

When they were gone, Dell threw the shovel. It crashed against the wall of the stall with a crack. What was he supposed to do?

Someone would remove the Rhodipus' from power. Wasn't that what was best for Madra? Probably.

He ran a hand through his grimy hair. Which side was Edmund on?

And did it matter?

Dell had never considered himself a political person. Since coming to the city, he'd kept his head down, taken everything his supposed family had done to him, and worked hard. When he was frustrated, he tended to slam his fists into people's faces as if he was a commoner rather than scheme and connive like the rest of the merchant class. Who was he kidding? He was a bastard. He couldn't be part of that class and that suited him fine.

And Edmund had seen something in that?

He pushed out a breath, unsure if he wanted to go to the meeting or not.

But really, what did he have to lose?

He had nothing.

He patted horse-Ian's nose and shuffled past him out of the barn. Edmund and Camille's carriage had created ruts near the gate that he'd no doubt have to fill.

If he was going to make it to Edmund's manor house,

he had to leave before his stepmother returned from the dressmakers.

He walked to the side of the barn where a stable hand always left the barrels of water he'd filled from the well. They replenished water buckets inside each of the animal stalls.

Dell gripped the sides of the tallest barrel and bent to plunge his head underneath the cool water. He raised it and flung dripping hair out of his face as the water soaked into the shoulders of his thin shirt. He scrubbed a hand over his face to remove the remaining dirt from a morning of work in the stables.

Now or never.

Time to decide.

He glanced at the large black iron gate behind him. Ominous spikes lined the top of the structure. They meant it as a warning to all others.

Don't try to beat the Tenyson's in business or in anything else. You won't win.

A carriage rumbled up the street and through the partially open gate. Dell's chest deflated as his stepmother appeared.

She scowled when she saw him.

"What are you doing, you worthless boy? Standing around? Those stables had better be mucked by lunch and then you're to head to the docks. One of our vessels has arrived, and you're to help in getting the goods to the warehouse."

Think, Dell. He flicked his eyes back to the barn.

"Something isn't right with moth—with the cow." He forced a concerned frown onto his face after almost calling the cow mother.

"What's this you're talking about?" she asked harshly.

The cow was the most prized possession they owned. In the mountainous Madra, only the wealthy had cows. Poorer folk kept goats. Some occasionally had a horse. But few had cows. And it was his ticket to that meeting.

He nodded, a frown turning his lips down. "She's not producing milk."

"It," his stepmother said. "The cow is not a person. Not a she. Why isn't it producing milk?"

"I don't know. We need to fetch Redden Martin."

"Then what are you waiting for? Take a horse and fetch the cow man."

By "cow man", she meant the one person they knew in Madra who worked with cows and kept them in good health. He lived in a small one-room shack across the city.

Dell ran into the barn, thankful his stepmother didn't follow him. She stayed out of the barn except when it came time to harass him.

He considered the full buckets of milk sitting outside the cow's stall; thankful he hadn't carried them to the house yet. Glancing out the door, he didn't see his stepmother, so he hauled the buckets two at a time to the small stream that ran behind the barn. The back wall of the estate had been built directly over it.

If anyone caught him dumping cow's milk, he'd be in serious trouble. It was worth too much in a city that lived on goat's milk, olives, and grapes. Meat could sometimes be hard to come by during wartime. Another consequence of the king's actions. Trade had grown more difficult. The merchants climbing the spiral were the ones who still seemed to be able to get their goods from kingdoms torn apart by fighting.

Once the milk was gone, he hurried to saddle Ian and climbed on. He kicked his heels into the horse's flanks and took off.

As a boy, he'd ridden his horse every day. The beast was the only thing of any value he and his mother owned. Since then, he had little opportunity to feel the wind whip through his hair. He swerved around people in the busy streets, passing Agathe's bakery with only a glance. She wanted him to join with Edmund. Why? He still couldn't wrap his head around the fact she'd known exactly who his father was.

And she hadn't cared.

She'd treated him like he truly belonged among the city-folk.

Agathe seemed to trust Edmund.

Trust didn't come easily to Dell. At all, really.

When he reached the more affluent ambassador's sector, Dell pulled the reins to slow horse-Ian. There was a representative from each of the five neighboring kingdoms living in the row of grandiose marble homes. No terracotta tiles adorned their roofs. Instead, they comprised an intricate thatching done meticulously. The street was deserted save for a few servants bustling in and out of doors.

This was one of the problems in Madra. The king spent the treasury on two things: The army and impressing his fellow rulers. Instead of increasing food supply for his own people, he showered these foreigners with ornate homes and feasts.

Once again, Dell didn't know which side he hoped Edmund was on. Did he want the royal family overthrown because their policies were destroying his kingdom? Or did loyalty to one's king mean more than that?

He steered the horse around to the back of the second house and slid down. They had left the back gate unlatched, and he opened it just wide enough to slide through, guiding the horse in after him.

He entered the courtyard on the other side, unsure what he should do next. His eyes scanned the flowering surroundings. It wasn't unlike the house his so-called family lived in. Why should he trust Edmund when he didn't trust them? Wealth was a disease. Those who had it lorded it over the rest and those who didn't worked their entire lives just for a taste.

That was the way of the city.

Dell longed for the simpler life in the mountain villages. His mother had been all he'd needed. His neighbors had nothing but the land they grew olives and grapes on. And they wanted little else. They hadn't needed much to be happy, unlike the people who now surrounded him in the city, constantly seeking more.

The heavy oak door that led into the house opened and a thickset man stuck his head out. "Good, you've arrived. Leave the horse. The stable boy will deal with him. Come."

As soon as Dell stepped into the house, he paused. The grandness was left outside, replaced by simple furnishings and little decoration. The wooden floor creaked underneath his feet as he walked into the living area.

The man turned to him. "The ambassador will be here in a moment. Would you like some wine?"

"N—" Dell cleared his throat. "No, thank you."

The man issued a short bow and retreated from the room.

It wasn't long before something thumped down the hall. Seconds later, Princess Camille appeared. Her serious face showed no warm greeting as she sighed. "Edmund…" She said his name with no emotion. "He just can't keep himself out of trouble. What about you, Dell? Are you prepared to get wrapped up in that man's insane ideas?"

"I—" What was he to say to that? He wanted no insanity in his life. Before Edmund, he was content working his fingers to the bone every day, getting the adrenaline rush of an occasional street fight, and then losing himself and his memories in his carvings. He touched the pocket sewn into his shirt where he always kept his carving knife and his latest wooden creation. In the past few weeks, he'd needed to be healed—again, pulled a knife on the crown prince, and spent time with the palace mistress while she was dressed as a boy—for whatever reason.

"I'm not sure," he finally admitted.

Camille sat in a chair opposite him. "Well, get sure. Edmund doesn't play games, boy. I've known him for years—hating him for most of them—and he never backs down from doing what he thinks is right."

There'd been little chance for Dell to do the right thing over the years. His brothers forced many poor situations on him. But his mother would have wanted him to stand up for something, to be more than a working grunt with no family.

She'd want him to put his faith in something.

He lifted his eyes to meet Camille's dark gaze. "I want to do right too."

She pursed her lips and nodded. "I know what it is to feel as if you have no family. Only, in my case, I was wrong. I didn't agree with my brother on a lot of things and betrayed him. But Alexandre forgave me. Do you know what I learned?"

Dell shook his head.

"Trust is the most valuable commodity in the six kingdoms. My brother married me off to remove me from the palace. He could have chosen an ogre of a man. Instead, he chose someone who was kind and loyal. My husband fought for my family with every breath. I didn't love him, but I always had faith in him. It's funny, Alex wanted to get rid of me and I ended up staying at the palace longer because of it."

Dell wasn't sure what this story had to do with him, so he let her continue.

"I regretted betraying my family—because it was the wrong thing to do for Gaule. But if it would have saved my kingdom, I'd do it again. No question."

Confusion creased his brow. "I don't understand."

Edmund's voice invaded their conversation. "Your family, Dell." He walked into the room. "They're going to overthrow the king and I need your help to stop them."

Dell rubbed his eyes. "I think I'll take that wine now."

EDMUND RETURNED from the cook-room balancing three cups of red wine.

Dell took his and gulped greedily before devolving into a fit of coughing as the wine hit his taste buds.

Edmund chuckled.

"I think I'm dying," Dell wheezed. "What is that?"

"Wine." Camille hid a smirk behind her cup.

When Edmund finished laughing, he explained. "In Bela and Gaule, we don't cut our wine with water as you Madrans do."

"Why the bloody hell not? That was horrid."

"You get used to it." Camille shrugged.

Edmund stood. "I'll get some of the olives I picked up at the market today. That should ease your Madran palate."

Dell lifted the cup to his lips again without thinking, but as soon as the wine hit his lips, he put it down and shook his head. "Doesn't the great ambassador of Bela have servants to fetch his food?"

Camille raised an eyebrow. "Do you know anything about him at all?"

Did he? Dell tried to recall any facts about Edmund. He was from Bela and claimed their king and queen as his friends. He had some sort of magic. Beyond that, Dell knew nothing at all.

Understanding lit in Camille's eyes. "Edmund isn't one to ask someone to do something he can accomplish himself. Your king supplies him with enough gold to hire a host of servants, but he lives as simply as he would in Bela."

"What about the man who greeted me when I arrived?"

Camille lowered her gaze. "From what Edmund told me, Bemus lost everything in a fire—including his family.

Edmund employs him merely as a means to give the man a home."

Edmund returned with a platter balancing on one hand. He glanced between Camille and Dell. Dell had always liked Edmund, but now he watched him with a new respect in his eyes.

Maybe Edmund wasn't as different as Dell thought.

"What?" Edmund asked as he set the cheese and olive laden tray on the table. "Is Camille spinning tales about me again? She used to not like me very much."

Camille laughed. "Used to?"

Edmund flashed her a grin before turning to Dell. All seriousness returned to his face.

His family. Dell pictured his stepmother and brothers. Were they truly conspiring against the king? A king who gave them everything. Lady Tenyson was the tip of the spiral, giving her untold power. She had the king's ear in all things. Rumors had even spread through the city that the princess' ball was merely a formality and it was Ian Tenyson she was to wed.

None of it made any sense.

Then the truth hit him and it hurt worse than he'd expected. He met Edmund's eyes. "This is why you befriended me. Why you've saved me time and again. Why I mean anything to you. I am a Tenyson. The only one you could get to." Dell stood. "You asked me to put my loyalty into you, but you've never reciprocated. Agathe, Mari, Corban… It's not me you want, only my name."

"Dell…" Edmund stepped toward him, but Dell held up a hand and Edmund froze.

"No, don't lie to me, Edmund. I've spent my life

around the likes of you. You take and take with no thought to who might be hurt. My family will supposedly betray the king, and you want me to what, spy on them? Risk my life? Because I guarantee if I'm caught, my life means nothing to them."

"Your king needs you, Dell Tenyson." Edmund's low voice rumbled through the room. "I once told you my life changed when I had something to fight for. Yours can too."

"I don't want to fight for the king!" The words were out before Dell could stop them. Heavy breath rattled through his chest. "Let the priests put me in a cell for treason, I don't care, but King Rhodipus will never have my loyalty."

He'd questioned himself so much when he hadn't known which side Edmund was on. Questioned his own loyalty to Madra, something he'd never thought of before. Could he support the king and the people both? Were they on the same side?

He didn't know.

The only thing he knew was he couldn't choose his stepmother or his brothers. If neither side held anything for him, what was his choice? There were only two sides, right? Either the king was overthrown, or he wasn't.

Edmund dropped his voice. "I'm not going to throw you in a cell, Dell. I'd never…" He pushed a breath past his teeth and ran a hand through his blonde hair.

Something else made little sense. Dell glanced toward the door, wanting to make his escape, but he didn't move. "You're not Madran, Edmund. Your true loyalty is to a king across the sea. Why are you fighting for King Rhodipus? Why are you spending your gold on spies instead of luxuries like the other ambassadors? Your life should be easy here. I need to understand you. What you're asking of me… not all of us have had the luxury of being able to put their faith in their king. I see what his wars do to this kingdom every single day. It's in the gaunt faces of the children begging for food from equally hungry sailors. It's in the war widows and the knowledge that many of this kingdom's young men will never set foot on our shores again. I know Madra aided Bela in its war with Dracon… is that enough for you? Because it isn't for me."

Throughout this exchange, Camille stayed silent, but she chose now to speak. "The boy's words hold weight, Edmund. I know why my loyalty is to the Rhodipus name. For the good of Gaule, I must wed Estevan and help him keep the throne. But I know you… I know what it is you fight for. It's never been about the crown, but the man who wears it. Why have you chosen this one?"

Edmund's jaw clenched, and he collapsed into a chair. He drained his wine and set the cup down with a heavy clang. "King Rhodipus is cruel, ambitious, and vile, but this world needs stability. Madra must remain at peace if we are to continue rebuilding Bela. We need their trade."

"No." Camille narrowed her eyes. "The Tenysons are merchants. They will ensure trade is not interrupted. There is something else."

Dell watched the fight leave Edmund's eyes. His lips turned down as a sigh inflated his muscular chest.

Dell crossed the room and put a hand on Edmund's shoulder. He faced the same dilemma as Dell. Protect a king who only hurt the kingdom, or let the royal family fall.

Edmund bent forward with his elbows on his knees. "I

believe in tradition," he started. "Not in the way Madrans do—with the priests protecting it. But real history and a future that furthers the kingdom's culture." He lifted his head to peer up at Dell. "Estevan Rhodipus is not his father. I've never been more sure of anything. The king doesn't hold my loyalty as you've said, but his son has every bit of it. Stev is going to save this kingdom. He will save us all."

Eight

Helena studied her eldest brother as he paced the length of the council chambers. His steps held the confidence only he possessed.

"You accept?" He stopped in front of Camille. "You will follow through with the betrothal?"

Camille nodded solemnly. "My kingdom needs this of me. They have assured me you are a man worthy of our alliance."

His shoulders relaxed, and he blew out a breath. "That's good news. Very good indeed." He peered into her eyes. "I promise you, Camille Durand, I will be a good husband to you. We will lead Madra into a golden age of prosperity and safety together."

The ambassador of Gaule stepped forward and clapped his hands together. He was a little man who'd had nothing to do with Camille since she set foot in Madra. But now he got his chance at being front and center, and he would not pass it up.

"Wonderful! This is fantastic. I am so pleased we

could come to an agreement. Now, we must discuss the details. Gaule needs troops and soon."

Helena's father chose then to intervene. "We have already begun preparations. After the ball, my son, Quinn will lead the men into Gaule. We will put these rebellions to bed."

"Fantastic." The ambassador scanned the room. "Maybe we should speak in private, your Majesty."

"Of course." The king shot a look around the room, and each person present knew the meaning without explanation.

Stev walked with Helena back toward the residence.

"I'm proud of you, brother." She smiled, her cheeks pushing up against the mask.

"For what?"

"For being the kind of prince another kingdom wants to tie themselves to. From what I've heard, Queen Catrine cares deeply for her children. Yet, she's willing to give her only daughter to Madra for your wife."

"Rulers do what they have to keep their kingdoms safe."

Helena touched his arm. "You're going to make a great king. I'm not sure I've told you that yet."

"Why do you say that?"

The crack in his confidence stunned Helena, but she didn't let it show. "I heard that a shipment of food meant for the palace, veered off the path and ended up in the Eastern part of the city. It quite upset father he couldn't have fresh berries for his crème yesterday. You wouldn't happen to know what caused the royal troops escorting the food to get lost on the way from the docks, would you?"

He shrugged. "Quinn was leading them. Ask him."

She laughed. "I did. He told me the idea came from higher up the food chain. I highly doubt father authorized it."

"It's not up to me to decide what you believe."

"Dammit, Stev." She yanked on his arm, pulling him to a stop. "Everyone knows you have a brilliant mind. Why don't you want them to know you have a heart as well? That you aren't..."

"Aren't what?"

Accusation shone in his eyes. She'd almost said he wasn't like their father. Cold. Calculated. Uncaring.

But she'd never spoken those words out loud.

The only thing Stev had in common with their father was his great mind and his ambition. But he wouldn't drain the treasuries and issue overbearing taxes for his determined ways. He knew enough not to follow the priesthood blindly.

"Nothing," she said quickly. "It's nothing, Stev. I just... I love you and one day you're going to fix us."

They'd reached the residence to find Cole and Quinn lounging on the red flowered couches. Kassander sprawled in front of a fireplace crackling with flames. Stev stopped at the edge of the room, uncertainty entering his gaze. It killed Helena that her brother didn't feel comfortable with the rest of them.

"I have business to attend to." Stev turned on his heel and marched back into the hall.

Kassander jumped to his feet and ran toward her. "Where is Stev going? He promised he'd take me for a ride today."

"I'm sorry, Kass." Helena gripped her brother's shoulder, truly feeling bad for the kid. He idolized Stev. Stev loved the youngest Rhodipus, but he didn't realize how much his sternness could cut sometimes.

Helena walked farther into the room. Cole still watched Stev's retreat, his eyes flashing with irritation. He shook his head as if returning to himself and smiled up at her.

Quinn moved over to create space and Helena sank into the couch between the twins.

"Camille has agreed to the betrothal."

Cole snorted in disgust. His feelings for Stev had always been plain.

Quinn wrapped an arm around her shoulders. "That's good news. Looks like it's certain I'll be headed to Gaule after the ball."

Helena laced her fingers with his and leaned her head on Cole's shoulder. Kass climbed up on Quinn's other side. Helena used her free hand to remove her mask.

No one made her feel as safe, as loved, as her brothers. Nothing could destroy her bond with them. Not tension with her father or the distance that was between them when the twins were off with the army. Not even Kassander's eventual role in the priesthood she hated so much.

Some small hope inside her thought maybe Stev would be the king to abolish the priesthood once and for all. Madra no longer needed their traditions and laws upheld. They didn't need the priesthood's harsh prison when the palace had unused dungeons. No future princess should have to wear a mask for her entire adolescence.

Unlike her father or his father before him, Stev had a

heart. Helena might be the only person he showed it to, but she knew it was there.

Each of her brothers kept secrets from the entire world, but she saw them. Quinn hated army life. He talked as if it was a grand adventure with travel and excitement. But he wanted more than anything to just fall in love and live quietly.

Kassander portrayed all the bravado of a young boy, but his future in the priesthood terrified him.

Cole wanted their father's approval despite his obvious disdain for the man. He wanted to be seen as his equal.

And Stev… well, Stev was good. Truly good in the way few people were.

Helena didn't know what they saw in her. False acceptance of her circumstances? Bravery in the face of an impending marriage—possibly to Ian Tenyson?

In truth, she wanted an adventure outside Madra. To be free from this palace, this life as the hidden princess.

Camille's appearance interrupted her thoughts. Sophia ushered the other princess into the room before returning to her duties.

Helena sat up, releasing her brothers. Camille watched the four of them longingly.

"Helena," she started. "Would you like to take a walk with me?"

Helena glanced at Cole in uncertainty. What did this cold princess want with her? And a walk? Camille could barely hobble around with that cane of hers. Surely it would be better for her to have tea in the sitting room. Then every restraint Helena had faced in her life came to mind. People always told her what she couldn't do because of tradition or because she was the princess. She refused to do that to Camille. If she thought a walk was best, who was Helena to tell her otherwise?

Cole nudged her from the couch, and it was only then she realized she hadn't yet given her answer. She rose to her feet with a nod. "A walk would be nice."

Quinn handed her the discarded mask, and she tied it to her face before following Camille from the room.

They walked in silence past the tapestries depicting Madran victories. They reached the door leading to the palace gardens where rows upon rows of flowers longed to bloom. A blast of chilly air rushed at them as they stepped onto the winding stone path that cut through the bushes and trees.

Helena rubbed her arms, wishing she'd thought to bring her cloak.

Camille, seemingly immune to the cold, continued forward, the clop of her cane the only sound between them.

"It's beautiful here." Camille's voice was so small, Helena almost thought she'd imagined it. She knew exactly what the princess meant. Camille spent the prior day in the city with Edmund and compared to the crowded, odorous streets, everything within the palace walls was perfect.

Only, Helena preferred the activity and life those streets possessed. She only grunted in response to Camille.

Camille spoke again. "I'm sorry if I've been… rude."

Helena stopped walking. "Madra may not be your home, but we invited you here to join us." She shook her head. "I've been surrounded by my brothers my entire life, and I love them, but they're… boys."

Camille laughed suddenly. "I know exactly how you feel. I haven't lived my life confined as you have, but sometimes it felt as though my brothers were my only companions."

"Boys are…"

"Gross?" Camille finished.

A smile flashed across Helena's face. "They do always seem to smell."

"Sometimes I wondered if Alexandre and Tyson even bathed." A fond smile settled on her lips. "Those are my brothers. We aren't close anymore. Too much has happened. But we once were."

"I can't imagine ever losing my bond with Stev, Quinn, Cole, or Kass."

"It's… hard." Camille glanced away.

"What's it like?" Helena had to know. "To be marrying someone in a different kingdom?"

Camille shrugged. "I may have only accepted the betrothal today, but I never really had a choice."

"I think it would be exciting. To venture somewhere new. But I'm second born. It's my duty to marry a Madran who will strengthen our power here."

"I'm glad you'll be staying." Camille began walking again. "I would like us to be friends."

"That would be nice."

"Tell me about Estevan."

A grin spread across Helena's face. "He likes to act as though he doesn't care about anything, but he does. So much. Stev is the best. His one weakness is my father. The king demands things of his heir that I know Stev doesn't agree with. He has to give the order to levy more taxes on the common folk and sometimes to reduce the import fees. Stev thinks it's a mistake putting more money in merchant hands and less in the pockets of the poor."

"So, the king controls him?"

"Except when it comes to me. Stev defies father to protect me from his wrath and also from the priests."

"Priests?"

"The order is charged with enforcing traditions by making them law. They change the laws rapidly and imprison anyone who doesn't comply until they can pay a rather large fee for their release."

"That's—"

"Horrible? Yes. Sometimes I wonder if it would be better to board a ship to Bela and marry some man there."

"The only Belaen man of consequence without a wife is Edmund." She snickered.

Helena scrunched up her face. "I don't care about that. I think I could be happy with a common man. As long as he was kind."

Camille opened her mouth to respond, but as they passed a purple flowering tree and breathed in its lavender scent, a scuffling sound came from around the corner followed by a soft groan.

"Someone's hurt." Helena picked up speed.

"Uh, that's not what it sounded like." Camille smirked as she tried and failed to catch up.

Helena rounded the corner and when the bushes no longer concealed the two other people present, she froze, her face going hot.

She should have left. Should have walked away before anyone knew she was there. But she couldn't move.

Camille finally caught up to her and a very unprincess-like snort left her. "Edmund!" she yelled. "First my brother and now my future husband?"

Edmund wrenched away from Stev who he'd been kissing moments before.

"Helena." Stev's eyes snapped to hers.

Helena shook her head and turned. Before she knew what was happening, she'd run the length of the gardens, seeking the safety of the palace.

"Len, wait!" Stev jogged after her and wrenched her arm back, forcing her to stop.

"Let me go, Stev."

"Not until you talk to me."

She twisted around so suddenly, he stepped back. "Talk to you about what? You're the heir to the throne. It's your duty to marry a foreign princess and have children. But you're… you're…"

All confidence had left her brother and she couldn't remember ever seeing him so unsure of himself.

"Len." His voice held a tortured note. "You know as well as I do Madran tradition is flawed. It takes and takes, leaving nothing of us behind. I can't…" He ran a hand through his dark hair.

Realization snapped into her. This was why he hadn't told her father of her journeys out into the city without her mask. He understood how little their duty afforded them.

Stev needed her now just as she'd needed him. That's what they'd always done: protected each other.

She reached out tentatively to take his hand. "I'm

sorry. I'm shocked… but you're my brother before you're the heir. At least in my mind. I won't tell anyone."

His posture sagged with relief. "Thank you."

"Do you love him?" She couldn't believe she was having this conversation with Estevan of all people. He'd always been so sure, so confident. What did she want him to say? No would mean he was risking everything for nothing. If the priests found out… But yes… That would mean all of this was real.

There was no law against a man loving another man in Madra. But there'd always been different rules for the royals than the commoners. A prince couldn't love anyone he wanted.

Stev, who rarely showed any kind of emotion, stared at her with glassy eyes. "I do. So much."

"How long?"

"What?"

"How long have you and Edmund…"

"Since right after they sent him here from Bela. At first, he was heartbroken because he'd left behind the man he'd thought he'd loved in Bela. I'd been having a hard time with some things father asked me to do. Edmund and I… we fixed each other."

As her shock faded away, she felt closer to Stev than she ever had. She squeezed his hand. "Now we just have to decide what to do about your betrothed."

He glanced over his shoulder to where Camille was berating Edmund. Her voice drifted toward them as they neared.

"Honestly Edmund," she said. "I don't know what to do with this." She put her hands on her head and turned to face Stev. "And you… ugh!"

"Camille." Helena observed her. She couldn't force her to honor the betrothal when they all now knew it meant a loveless marriage. But weren't most arranged marriages the same? "What do you want to do here?"

She groaned. "I need to sit down." Hobbling across the garden, she dropped onto a limestone bench. After a moment, she lifted her head to find them all watching her.

Helena wouldn't tell the king… but she didn't know what Camille would do.

The Gaulean princess pushed out a breath. "I will still marry you, Estevan." Her shoulders sagged under the weight of this new knowledge. "Gaule needs this from me. And Madra needs to never find out about you two. You must end this. Now." She pierced Edmund with one final look before stalking toward the door and disappearing from view.

Silence descended as Helena glanced from Stev to Edmund and back again. "She's not wrong. I'm sorry, but you have to know this can't continue. If it had been father who found you…" She tugged her dark hair over one shoulder to fiddle with the ends. "I'm scared, Stev."

Estevan didn't move, but Edmund reached for her and pulled her into a hug. "It will be okay, Len."

Helena pressed her face into his firm chest as he stroked her hair. "This is Madra." Her mask scratched against her face, bringing it to the forefront of her mind. A door opened behind them and a pair of priests in their sweeping white robes invaded the privacy of the garden. Tears hung in Helena's lashes, refusing to fall. "Nothing is ever okay."

Nine

No Madran princess ever forgot their eighteenth name day.

It meant they were one step closer to being rid of the mask for good.

Celebrations would stretch on for an entire week, beginning with the Madran games and cumulating in the ball where the mask would be removed once and for all.

Helena woke before the sun as anticipation twisted her gut. Today, she'd be allowed to be among the people. Not as the boy she'd pretended to be on her trips into the city, but as herself.

The jaunt to the docks to greet Camille had been her first journey outside the palace walls since she was a child—at least sanctioned journey. But she'd gone from palace steps to carriage to docks before returning to the carriage. There'd been no time to soak in the energy of the Madran people.

She sat up in her carved mahogany bed, lifting her

eyes to the silk canopy overhead. They had given her everything. Her life lacked no luxuries.

Why had she never been happy within these walls?

Maybe for the same reason Stev hadn't been. Under the watchful eyes of their father, they could never let their desires shine through.

The shock of seeing Stev and Edmund together had worn off, replaced by guilt. How had she not seen it before?

Had she known her brother at all?

The answer to that was simple. No one knew Stev Rhodipus. He made sure of it. She hugged her arms across her chest, hoping he at least let Edmund see who he truly was.

And who he wasn't.

Estevan Rhodipus was not their father and he never would be.

Sometimes Helena thought she was the only one who saw that.

Twisting her tangled hair over one shoulder, she slid from the bed and padded to the window. Pushing open the glass panes, she sucked in a deep breath of the chilly morning air.

What was this week going to bring for her?

Was it all a formality when her father could force her into a marriage with Ian Tenyson?

The silent courtyard below her window was awash in silver moonlight as she leaned out to scan her eyes across the palace grounds. In the distance, beyond the palace walls, the city would wake soon and prepare.

The Madran games, held every four years, were sacred. All those who were able, crowded into the circular arena at the edge of the city to watch events such as boxing matches, javelin throwing, and discus.

Any man who wanted to be considered a suitor for the princess' hand competed, hoping to show their abilities.

On the horizon, the sun battled with the moon, day wanting dominance over night.

Helena shut the window just as the door to the room connected to hers opened. Sophia emerged and froze.

"Princess, I was expecting to have to wake you this morning."

Helena offered a small smile. "Just basking in the last moments of the day's peace."

The old woman's face softened. "Do not be afraid, child."

How did Helena explain it wasn't fear coursing through her this morning, but something else entirely? Acceptance. Resignation. She'd marry a Madran man and live within the palace for the rest of her days. Estevan would wed Camille and one day become king. Madra would struggle along as a warring kingdom. Nothing was going to change.

And today, they'd look into the faces of common people who never had enough to eat. Wealthy merchants would mingle with those working for them who barely survived.

And all the while, the already empty treasury would pay for the extravagance.

But she was Helena Rhodipus. She couldn't voice any of that.

"I'll try not to be," she said instead.

Sophia's face creased in understanding, when in reality, she didn't understand at all.

A knock sounded on the door.

Sophia unlatched it and let the queen into the room.

Helena instantly relaxed under her mother's comforting gaze.

"It's quite early." Her mother raised a brow. "Whoever had the idea to start the games at such an hour deserves an arrow right between the eyes." She tapped her forehead.

"Mother!" Helena gasped, trying to muffle a laugh as Sophia shot them both disapproving looks.

The queen only shrugged. "I have yet to have my morning tea. I'm allowed to be a bit grumpy."

"Your Majesty." Sophia crossed her arms, staring at the queen as if she were naught but a child. "A better example must be set around children."

"Oh yes." Helena's mother met the older woman's gaze. "I like teaching my daughter—who is no child—to have humor in her life." She gestured to the door. "Helena and I would appreciate some tea."

Sophia shook her head and scuffled from the room.

Helena grinned. "You really should be nicer to her, mother."

"My dear, that woman has been with us a long time and I don't remember a single smile gracing her lips." She crossed the room, stopping directly in front of Helena. "Happy name day, my sweet." Putting a hand on each of Helena's cheeks, her mother kissed the top of her head.

When she pulled back, there were tears in her hazel eyes.

"Mother, what is it?"

The queen shook her head, tight black curls bouncing with each movement. "I'm just a silly old woman. You're my girl. It's difficult to think of giving you to anyone else, even if you will still be in the palace."

Helena took her mother's hand. "Would you help me prepare today?"

She wiped her face. "That would be lovely."

Sophia returned with a tea tray laden with fresh mugs, mint leaves, and hot water along with grapes and biscuits.

Once Helena had eaten and bathed, her mother helped her into the gown she's chosen for her. Thankfully, there was no corset, but the wide yellow skirt still made it difficult to move. As her mother and Sophia pinned her hair in an intricate design of curls and loops, she ran her hands over the white lace of the bodice.

When they finished, it was time for the royal family to make their journey to the arena.

Sophia handed Helena an ivory mask with wide ribbons. Beautiful didn't begin to describe it, but as she set it against her olive-tone skin, all magnificence faded, leaving only the heavy weight of confinement behind.

The boys were waiting at the carriage when they arrived. Quinn and Cole wore the red blazers of their officer's uniforms with fitted linen pants. They would exchange those for their boxing gear when they joined in the games.

Kassander looked like a mini version of Stev who stood rigidly by the rear of the carriage. His black coat was emblazoned with the triangular family crest. He shifted his stance and Kass imitated him.

Helena shook her head, a smile coming to her lips.

It dropped when her father descended the steps without a word to any of his children. Cole glared and Helena reached for him. "Don't let him see how he affects you."

Cole relaxed and slid an arm around Helena's shoulders. "You look beautiful. Happy name day."

She stretched up to drop a kiss on his cheek and crowded into the royal carriage with the rest of the family.

Streams of people made their way to the arena and by the time the royal family arrived, it was already bustling with activity.

The horses stopped at the king's private entrance where a troop of palace guards lined up and waited for them. Their father got out first and went ahead without a glance back at them. Stev lifted Kassander out while Quinn and Cole held hands up to Helena and her mother.

Together, they followed the king through the small gate. A dim tunnel led to a platform above the arena floor.

Helena froze when she stepped onto the platform. She'd never seen so many people. Her eyes scanned the rows of seats stretching out in a circle. They had divided the arena floor into separate areas for different events.

A horn blew, its sound reverberating around the stone structure. All activity ceased as the crowd lifted their eyes to the royal family.

The king stepped forward. "Welcome!"

Helena wondered if any besides those wealthy enough to be seated near the platform could hear him.

"Today is a great day for Madra," he continued. "You have all gathered here to celebrate what we have accomplished as a kingdom. Through many hard battles, we have gained power throughout the six kingdoms."

"Power means nothing without food," someone yelled.

Helena craned her neck to find the man who'd shouted, but two royal guards obscured her view as they rushed down the aisle. It happened so quickly, she didn't react. They pulled the man from his seat and dragged him toward a line of priests who stood ready to act.

The king went on as if none of it had happened. "Today we mark the eighteenth year of my daughter. May I present, in her first official appearance, princess Helena Rhodipus."

The king stretched his arm back to gesture her forward, but her feet froze.

"Len," Stev hissed. "Go."

Her mother took her arm and led her into the light. "Wave, dear."

Helena lifted a hand and waved to her people for the first time.

A cheer wound through the crowd as they caught their first glimpse of the hidden princess. What stories had been told of her? She wondered.

As they continued to cheer, confidence bloomed within her. She belonged to them. Not to her father. To the people.

And she wouldn't let them down.

She cleared her throat. "Let the Madran games begin."

Ten

Dell slipped through the arena entrance, lost among the crowd of commoners using this entrance. His family would have used the merchant's gate, which allowed them to sit in proximity to the king.

He was glad for that because they'd forbidden him to come.

He walked straight for the boxing area, longing to get his chance at a fight. Madran tradition said the princess could choose any man common or merchant, to wed, but everyone knew that wasn't true and they allowed only those of quality to put their name in the draw.

A man bumped into Dell, jostling him as he rushed forward.

Orlo.

Dell's fists clenched, and he counted backward in his head. Fighting an unsanctioned fight in the king's presence would mean imprisonment.

Orlo glanced over his shoulder as if seeing Dell for

the first time. "Your minder not here to keep you out of trouble, boy?"

"You don't want my kind of trouble, Orlo. How is Catjsa?"

The bigger man scowled. "I wouldn't mind knocking you silly again. Name the place."

Dell opened his mouth to speak, but Edmund entered his mind. Dammit, he wanted to accept the fight, to be able to hit something.

Why couldn't he?

Because Edmund had it in his head to save a king who shouldn't be saved?

Because he was so sure Estevan would be a better ruler than his father?

Dell clenched his teeth, wanting to yell, wanting to go back to being just an unwanted son working himself to death.

Back to the quiet life of a nobody.

Your family is going to overthrow the king, and I need your help.

He wished he could ignore those words. But despite his effort, something inside him trusted Edmund in a way he'd trusted no one before.

He realized he still hadn't responded to the man who was now looming over him with a question in his eyes.

Dell sighed. "No, Orlo. I'm not going to fight you. Not today."

Orlo grunted. "Kid finally got some sense." He turned without another word and lumbered away.

Dell returned to watching the fight before him as the boxers lunged at each other. He started walking again toward the outer ring of the arena where the city's shopkeepers had set up booths. Agathe sold pastries to those who could pay and gave them to those who couldn't.

Dell pushed through the crowd of merchants, recognizable in their finer clothes.

Agathe's haggard face transformed when she saw him, and a smile stretched her lips. "Dell. I didn't think you'd be attending today."

Dell shrugged. "I just have to avoid my brothers. My step-mother declined the invitation because she doesn't want to surround herself with 'common folk'."

Agathe shook her head. "That woman…"

"Yeah. Listen, have you seen Edmund? I need to talk to him."

"Is he with the royal family?" She pointed a long finger toward a raised platform.

Dell's eyes passed over the king and narrowed. He didn't know what to think of Prince Estevan. The queen sat in her wing-backed golden chair with all the grace they knew her for. Unlike the other royals, she made an effort to help city-folk by handing out food.

The twins were mostly unknowns. They hadn't grown up in the public eye and now spent much of their time leading units of the army overseas. The young Prince Kassander had a grin on his face you couldn't help but reflect back at him.

Sitting beside him was the reason they were all there. It wasn't the first time Dell had seen the princess. He'd been shocked when she appeared with her mother at the docks. Even though he'd made a fool of himself, he'd needed to get a closer look at her, to see what was under those pretty masks.

Then, she'd laughed with him. Now, she looked… uncomfortable.

A frown tugged at the corners of her delicate painted lips. She was so close as the platform sat right near the boxing matches, yet her dark eyes said she wasn't there at all.

The king leaned across his wife and said something to the princess. Her spine snapped straight, and she pasted a fake smile on her lips.

A boxing match ended with one contestant unconscious. As someone dragged him away, they drew a new name.

"Orlo Willard," they called before pulling out another. "Ian Tenyson."

Dell reared back as he tried not to grin. He shrank away from the boundary line to hide himself among the crowd so Ian didn't see him.

Orlo paced the length of the square, waiting.

When Ian finally appeared, Dell sucked in a breath. A bandage held his arm to his chest. When had he been injured?

Ian turned to the crowd, sleazy charm oozing from every orifice. "I am honored to get my turn against this noble man." He nodded toward Orlo. "As a member of the merchant class, I'm ashamed to say I must invoke an old rule. If a competitor cannot compete due to injury or illness, they can uphold their honor should they appoint someone to fight in their name."

Reed appeared next to Dell. "Sorry, brother."

"About what?" Dell glanced sideways at him.

Ian continued. "I choose a fighter with much skill who

will uphold my family honor because it is his honor as well."

No. Dell shook his head and took a step back. Reed grabbed his arm.

"My brother." Ian's stare burned into Dell. "Dell Tenyson."

Reed shoved him across the boundary line. Dell stumbled before righting himself and glaring at Ian.

Ian smirked. "All of your city friends will know exactly who you are, brother." He said the last word as if it was a curse. "Your fate now rests with ours, Dell. Maybe that will help you choose a side."

Dell's eyes widened. They knew of his meeting with Edmund.

And they'd just told all of Madra he was one of them.

They'd claimed him and entwined his future with theirs.

Crap.

Eleven

The announcers voice rose into the air and Helena lurched forward in her seat.

"Dell Tenyson will serve as Ian Tenyson's second."

No, she couldn't have heard that right. *Tenyson?*

Dell was one of them? Disbelief coursed through her and she couldn't take her eyes from the boxing ring.

The boy she'd found fighting in the center of the city, who she'd worried over, was the son of the tip of the spiral? She'd never have spent time with him if she'd known.

Something didn't add up. His threadbare clothes and utter lack of manners… what was she missing?

Her eyes found Dell as they hustled him to the changing area. The lords who fought in that ring arrived at the games in fine clothing that spoke of wealth. They wouldn't risk dirtying it in a fight.

But Dell… had Edmund known? Of course he did. Edmund seemed to know everything that happened in Madra. That would explain how he'd known Dell.

But what about Mari and Corban? What did two magic folk have to do with the son of such a powerful family?

Dell's blonde hair shone as the sun beat down into the arena. He disappeared around the corner and Helena barely breathed until he returned.

Dell Tenyson.

The crowd cheered as he smiled up at them with an ease in his posture that hadn't been present in the other lords. He'd changed into linen pants cut off at the knees. He lifted his arms into the air, his bare chest straining with each movement.

"Honey," her mother said to her father. "Did you know there was a third Tenyson boy?"

Her father grunted. "Of course." But his eyes held more truth than his words. It was a shock to him as well. One thing was certain, the king's guards would be looking into the situation immediately when the fight ended.

Cole shifted in his seat, his eyes darting away from their father. He had to have known. He was closer to the Tenysons than his own parents.

"You knew Dell was Ian's brother, didn't you?" she asked.

Cole fixed her with a wary stare. "And how is it that my sister who has left the palace twice in her life knows a commoner like Dell?"

She refused to answer his question. "Apparently, Dell isn't a commoner at all."

Her brother snorted. "Of course he is. He doesn't even sleep in the great house. Lady Tenyson puts him with their common workers in the barn loft. He's the result of his father's unfaithfulness. Nothing more."

Helena stood to get a better look as the boxers faced each other. Instant recognition raced through her when she caught sight of the second man.

What had Edmund called him?

Orlo.

She shook her head, muttering to herself. "This isn't good." Dell was going to get himself killed.

Ian Tenyson stood next to the boundary line, a grin stretching his face. A shiver shot down her spine. Something wasn't right with that man.

Why was Orlo even in the fight? He had a wife. He wasn't competing to impress the royal family and hoping to win the princess—win her.

No, something else brought him here.

Ian.

It was the only explanation.

She had to get down there. Had to see him.

Turning to her father, she dropped her eyes. "Father, may I be allowed to go to the privy?"

He didn't take his eyes from where a man launched a javelin on the opposite side of the arena. "Tell the guards at the door to escort you."

"I would rather it be Quinn." She fluttered her eyelashes and dropped her lips into a worried frown. "I feel much safer in his presence."

"Sure, fine. Return promptly. The people need to see you enjoying the games."

Quinn gave her a questioning look as he collected his bag and rose to lead her through the door.

"Sir," one of the guards started. "Wait here. I'll have a few of my men take you where you need to go."

Helena gave a slight shake of her head, her eyes imploring Quinn to help her.

Quinn put a congenial hand on the guard's shoulder. "If I can't keep my sister safe, no one can."

The guard relaxed his stance. "Yes, sir."

Quinn grabbed Helena's elbow and pulled her away from the guards at the door. She stumbled, but he kept her from falling.

"Len Rhodipus." He sighed as he pulled her around the corner into a quiet hall. No one was allowed in this part of the arena while the royal family sat on their platform. He released her and pushed a hand through his dark hair. "What is this about?"

Quinn was the only member of her family who might allow her to do as she wished. She'd picked him specifically. Stev wouldn't even think of it and Cole would demand he go with her.

She rushed out a breath and met his eyes, unblinking. "I need to go down there."

"Where?" The caution in his voice told her he knew exactly where.

"The arena floor."

"Absolutely not."

"I'm not asking you, Quinn. It'll be easier with your help, but I've done it on my own before."

"Len." He lifted his eyes to the ceiling.

"Please, Quinn. Today is my name day. By the end of the week, I'll be tied to a man we all know won't be of my choosing. This mask…" She touched the soft fabric on her face. "It'll be gone but the cage will remain. You always speak to me of the freedom you experience when you leave the palace for other kingdoms. Let me feel that. Just once more. Please."

"You can't be gone long," he finally said.

A grin spread across her face. "So, you'll help me?"

"You have to promise you'll come back as quickly as you can. I can buy you some time, but not much. I'll tell father you fell ill and needed to collect yourself. He won't question it."

The truth stood between them. Their father wouldn't care if she fell ill as long as she eventually returned.

Quinn went on. "I'm going to station a guard I trust outside the privy so father believes it. You can go taste your freedom for a few minutes and then come right back. I'm sending one of my men down there to keep an eye on you."

"That's not—"

"Negotiable."

"Fine."

"I would rather accompany you. It would make me feel better."

Helena touched his arm. "But I'm not going as the princess so I can't really have the prince with me, can I?" She gestured to his bag. "I know you don't fight shirtless like Dell does. Let's see what I have to work with."

He reached in and pulled out long wool pants and a shirt she was going to drown in.

"More complicated than borrowing from Kass," she grumbled.

Quinn laughed and gestured to the privy door nearby.

Helena left her brother in the hall and stepped into the small washroom. As soon as the door slammed shut behind her, she pulled at the laces on the front of her dress, thankful her mother hadn't forced a corset on her. She slipped the knife, her constant companion, from her bodice and wiggled out of the gown. As she slipped Quinn's clothes on, she sighed at the comfort.

The pants tried falling to her knees, so she knotted them at the waist and rolled them until her feet were visible. The shirt hung off her small frame as if it was meant for an ape. She guessed it was, thinking of Quinn's bulk. She tucked it into her pants, knowing she probably looked like one of the homeless boys begging at the docks.

Her fingers ran under the bottom of the mask and she hesitated before untying it.

Pins dropped to the ground as she pulled them from her hair. She used the last few to pull her long curls back into the low tail worn by many sailors.

As she stepped from the room, Quinn held in a laugh and handed her a cloak.

"Where did you get this?" she asked. It was a thin linen, worn mostly by commoners.

"One of the guards." He shrugged as he eyed her curiously. "I thought Stev was joking when he told me before, but you really could pass for a young man."

"Just what every woman wants to hear."

He leaned in. "Those trying to disguise themselves should be pleased with the observation."

She started down the hall and turned to her brother once more. "Quinn… thank you."

"Any time, little sister. If there's one thing I've learned through years of war, it's that freedom is often more important than safety or tradition."

She smiled once more as she rounded the corner.

That was why she'd gone to Quinn for help. He understood.

She raced through the back hall until she found the door leading to the rest of the arena. A guard stood to one side, but he barely glanced at her, probably assuming she was a servant. They were worried about people coming in, not leaving.

That could be a problem for her, but she didn't stop to think about her return.

The crowd enveloped her as soon as she stepped onto the arena floor under the open sky. They wrapped her in their excitement. Their cheers vibrated through her bones. Adrenaline shot through her heart. This was what the royal family missed up on their platform.

Down here, among the people, there was life.

She nudged her way through the throng until she came upon the boxing match she'd needed to see up close. Was Corban here in case Dell needed him?

Sweat dripped between the ridges of Dell's abs and Helena's cheeks warmed as she remembered the day at the river. The day she hadn't been able to stop thinking about.

Right before Dell risked himself trying to protect her from Stev.

A crunch ripped through the air as Orlo's fist connected to Dell's jaw. The crowd cheered, rooting for Orlo. He was one of the few fighters who was one of them and not a merchant.

Helena shrank back as Dell reeled from the impact, his eyes connecting with hers as blood flew from his mouth.

An old woman beside her gasped. "That poor boy."

Helena couldn't help herself as she pulled the hood of the cloak farther around her face and turned to the woman. "You know the boxers, ma'am?"

She nodded, wiping a tear from under her eye. "Dell is such a sweet boy. Those brothers of his on the other hand…" She clamped her mouth shut as if she'd said something she shouldn't.

"Len." Dell's voice had Helena snapping her eyes to his. Orlo had retreated for a moment.

Crimson blood trickled from a cut on his brow, but he smiled.

He'd heard Stev call her Len, and it was too close to her real name, to all her secrets, but as she looked into the hazy eyes of the man before her, she didn't care.

Orlo stalked toward him.

"Be careful, Dell," she said.

He winked. "Always, darling." He twisted around to duck the next attack.

Helena should have left right then. She'd gotten the taste of excitement she'd wanted and her family would look for her.

But she couldn't move as Dell's knees struck the ground.

Twelve

Heat radiated up from the sandy arena floor as Orlo drove Dell onto his back.

The loss felt so familiar. Yet, this time, he had a bigger audience. The crowd had chosen to support Orlo since he was one of them. Dell never had been, and now they knew it.

A cheer wound around the arena. "Orlo! Orlo! Orlo!" Only the merchants stayed quiet.

Orlo raised his arms to the crowd, basking in their adoration. He was about to beat the son of the highest merchant in Madra.

"What do we have here?" Ian's voice pushed all fog from Dell's mind.

He spared a moment to find his brother and… he noticed her. Dammit, Len! He'd told her that disguise wouldn't work if anyone looked closely. And Ian had.

The eldest Tenyson had the eyes of a hawk, and they'd targeted Len, the girl Dell still knew too little about.

"No," he roared as he rolled to his feet, pain slicing through him at the movement.

He ran for Orlo, catching him around his thick waist and driving him into the ground. The momentary shock was all he needed to bring his fist down on the other man's face.

Ian would not touch Len, but if Dell was to stop it, he had to win this fight first. To end it.

He beat down on Orlo with a ferocity he'd never experienced before, anger rushing through him.

His chest heaved as he shoved himself off the still man.

Orlo raised an arm laboriously.

He conceded.

Shock pierced into Dell. He'd won.

But he didn't have time to soak in the sound of his name now roaring through the crowd. With every bit of strength he had left, he sprinted toward his brother who had a grip on Len's arm.

"Come on, sweetheart," Ian cooed. "I'll show you a good time."

"Let me go." Ice laced her voice.

"I don't think so."

Len narrowed her eyes seconds before twisting in his grasp, pulling a knife free of a sheath at her waist, and pointing it at him. She pulled on the bandage around his other arm. It came loose easily and Ian used his supposedly injured arm to slap her.

Dell jumped for them, wrenching his brother back. "Don't touch her," he growled.

"So much for being injured." She rubbed her cheek and raised her voice. "Looks like someone wanted to avoid fighting for his own honor. The princess will never choose a coward."

Ian glared up at the royal platform. The princess no longer sat in her seat and he shook his head. "I can ruin you, girl. Commoners like you are a scourge on this kingdom."

"And merchants like you destroy everything you touch."

He leaned closer and before Dell could stop him, he pressed his lips to hers. Dell shoved himself between them but not before Ian yelped and jumped back. "She bit me." He searched their surroundings. "Guards. This woman assaulted me."

Assaulting a merchant—whether or not you did it—had strict penalties.

Dell took Len by the arm. "Want to get out of here?"

Her eyes flicked to the king, indecision warring in her gaze. She flipped the knife in her hand and shoved it back into the sheath, giving him a nod.

Guards ran toward them and Dell pulled Len into a run. He never lost his grip on her hand as they weaved their way to the arena gates and out into the city. Heavy footsteps sounded behind them.

"The stables," Dell said, changing direction. He pulled Len along as her short legs struggled to keep up. Her breaths came out in harsh pants.

Behind the arena sat the largest stables in the city. Only merchants had the privilege of using them. They slowed to a walk. Dell glanced over his shoulder. The guards had stopped at the gates of the arena, not bothering to chase them.

The guard at the stable door eyed him curiously

before recognition lit in his eyes. Ian and Reed had made Dell bring their horses to the stables. He wound through the rows of stalls, making sure Len was still behind him.

Horse-Ian lifted his head as Dell stepped in front of him. "Alright, ye old bastard, we need to get out of here."

Horse-Ian snorted as his lips pulled back to show his teeth.

Dell swung the worn wooden stall door open and lifted the saddle from where it hung on a brass hook.

"Hurry," Len whispered, throwing a glance toward the door.

Dell didn't understand why she was so worried. They wouldn't come after two people who didn't matter.

Dell listened for any sign of the guards. "We'll be fine," he said.

"Are you sure?"

"You're the one who seems to have skill with that knife of yours." He lifted a brow. "You can just fight them off."

Her mouth dropped open.

A laugh burst out of Dell. "I'm kidding. We'll be fine, but if it makes you feel better, we can change our appearances. They'd look for a shirtless man and someone in a hood, give me your cloak."

She didn't hesitate as she unclasped it and shrugged it off. Hair broke free of the pins binding it to her head, giving her a wild look.

Her clothes spoke of a commoner but her smooth olive skin lacked the damage most Madrans suffered from working in the sun.

As her fingers brushed his, he felt no callouses.

He shook off his momentary stupor and fastened the

cloak at the neck. Gesturing to the horse, he said, "Up you go."

Her eyes flicked from the horse to his face and back again. "I've never…"

Even after a decade among the sea of buildings, he'd never get used to city-folk. "Let me guess, you've only ridden in carriages, not astride a horse."

Shame lit in her eyes, and his face softened. "Come on, princess. I'll be right behind you."

She froze, her eyes widening as she took a step back.

Guilt instantly struck him. "I'm sorry, miss. Ah…" He rubbed the back of his neck. "I won't call you princess again. That wasn't very nice."

Her shoulders relaxed. "Okay, but if I fall off…"

"You'll send your lover after me?" Why couldn't he control his own words? All manners had left his mind. His mother would have been ashamed. So what if she was the prince's mistress? She could still use a friend.

In truth, the prince could get her out of trouble with the guards, but Dell didn't say that. He wasn't ready to let her go back to her life yet.

He set his hands on her slim waist and lifted her onto the horse. Horse-Ian took a step back and Len yelped.

"Hey," Dell cooed to the beast. "Shhh… she's a friend." The horse glared at him as if saying *But what are you?*

Dell swung up behind Len and kicked the horse's flanks. They left the barn to no sign of pursuit—just as he'd thought. He should have ridden toward the palace to return Len to her rightful place.

He should have done a lot of things.

Instead, he gripped her tighter. "We can't let them

find us until this blows over. My brother has a long reach."

Only part true.

"I..." Len sputtered. "I need... to get back. They'll be looking for me." She seemed to hesitate for a moment. "But I can't. Not yet. Go."

Relieved he didn't have to deliver her home quite yet, Dell kicked the horse, and they took off through the deserted streets of the Madran capital. They had shut everything down for the games. As if a reminder, a twinge of pain stabbed through Dell's abdomen and he flinched.

"Are you okay?" Len asked.

"Fine." He gritted his teeth.

Normally, he'd head straight for Mari's shop to see if Corban could ease his pain. But he wanted to feel every bit of what his brother did to him this time.

Dell loved boxing, but fighting Orlo was a different kind of battle and Ian had known that. It was why he'd arranged it.

Hatred for his brothers burned in him. One day, he'd be free of him. He'd be free of all of them.

DELL'S GRIP on Helena grew weaker by the moment and she feared he'd slip right off the horse.

"We have to get you to Corban," she said.

"No." His large hand squeezed her side. "Keep riding."

The warm breath on the back of her neck sent a chill over her. Helena had never been so close to a man who wasn't related to her… other than Edmund, but he might as well be a relative.

What was her family thinking now? The princess disappeared from the Madran Games being held in her honor. Soon, the city would be in an uproar looking for her. Quinn would never trust her again after she broke her promise.

But for the first time in her life, she felt like something other than the caged bird she'd been all her life. She wasn't slinking through the streets on her own as she had before. This time, she rode proudly with a man whose very touch caused the hair on her arms to stand on end.

Dell wasn't like anyone she'd ever met. While wearing her mask, she'd entertained many of the city's merchants at the palace. The young men thought much of themselves, always preening and taking great care with their appearance. They'd cared more about being able to say they spent time in the princess' presence than actually paying her any attention.

It was why the Madran Games intrigued her. Those same men were put into a fight where skill mattered more than appearance. Any man of station in Madra trained in boxing from a young age. But training in your own courtyard differed greatly from facing crowds of common folk who wanted to see you hurt.

Dell… he was quick on his feet, but had been no match for Orlo's strength—until he saw Ian with her.

Why did he feel the need to protect her?

He still thought she was a prince's mistress for priest's sake.

Madra was not like the other kingdoms she heard about from stories. People of differing stations didn't look out for one another. They didn't join the army out of some pride for their king and country. Those who fought did so because it was an alternative to an empty belly.

She had no illusions about the people's loyalty to her father.

The closer to the edge of the city they drew, the farther apart the buildings became. The poorest city folk lived on the outskirts in one room shanties that would blow over the next time a big storm came ashore.

Her brothers would have averted their eyes, but her mother would meet the eye of every person they passed. She lifted her chin and smiled at the first old man they saw.

"Why isn't he at the games?" she whispered to Dell.

Dell's voice vibrated against her hair. "I know you live in the palace with your… with the royal family… but not everyone has the luxury of being able to comply every time the king says jump. Take a closer look at him."

The old man lifted his face to the sun, but it wasn't his weathered face or vacant eyes that caught her attention. As he shifted where he sat on the ground, his ripped trouser leg fluttered, twisting over where his right leg should be.

A tiny gasp escaped her.

"You really know nothing of Madra, do you?" Dell's voice held no judgment, only curiosity.

Helena shrugged as she dug her fingers into the horse's coarse mane, needing to feel the life underneath her fingers.

She needed to return to the palace before they tore the kingdom apart searching for her, but her chest tightened at the thought.

"Have you ever seen the sea, Len?"

Of course she hadn't. The only body of water she'd ever laid eyes on was the river that ran the length of the city, leading boats to the open sea between Madra and Bela.

"Len?"

She sighed. "No."

"Outside the city, there's a place where the river runs shallow enough to cross. A cove sits nearby where the sea washes ashore. Can I take you there?"

She closed her eyes, needing to say no. Her entire life, she'd obeyed the laws of Madra, following everything the priests told her to do.

Their faces came to her mind. White robes. Permanent sneers. The image changed to that of Kassander one day taking his position among them. Her sweet brother. Would the royal children ever be allowed to have something for themselves?

"Yes," she answered, realizing if she wanted good in her life, she'd have to take it and live with the consequences as they came.

Dell kicked the horse into a trot and before long, open land stretched before them, rolling and dipping all the way to the mountains in the distance.

Helena scanned the horizon, amazed by the beauty that existed beyond the crowded city. She shifted in the saddle, not even her sore bottom could distract her from the splendor of her kingdom.

This was her family's land. When her father spoke of his wars preventing invasions by keeping their enemies weak, he was protecting much more than what lay within the palace walls.

For the first time in her life, she understood him.

They passed into a thicket of trees and came upon a wide length of the river. The water ran swiftly toward the city.

A deer dipped its head to drink.

"Quiet," Dell whispered.

Helena had only ever seen deer in storybooks, but here she was in front of one.

Sensing their presence, the animal snapped its head up, wide brown eyes meeting theirs seconds before it dashed into the trees with a crash of branches.

Dell nudged the horse forward until he stepped into the water. Helena held her breath, hoping it was really as shallow as Dell believed.

She released it when they made it to the other side only to be greeted by a wall of moss-covered rock.

She scanned the impediment where it loomed over them, her shoulders deflating.

Dell, showing no signs of disappointment that he'd led them the wrong way, slid from the horse. He winced as his feet hit the ground.

"Dell." Helena tried to slide down as he had but her foot got stuck in the stirrup sending her twisting and tumbling to the ground. The impact sent a jarring force through her. Her foot still in the stirrup, it hung above the rest of her body.

The horse stepped away from her, dragging her slowly.

Dell jumped forward and wrestled her foot free. "You okay?" He bit back a laugh.

Helena rolled to her feet and scanned her body for any sign of blood. "You wouldn't be laughing if I'd died."

"You're right."

He grinned.

"Stop it."

"No."

"Dell."

"Len."

She punched his arm, and all joking faded from his face as pain invaded his eyes.

"Dell, you need to sit down." She touched his back as gently as she could. "Come on. Then we can find our way back to the city."

"We're not going back before you lay eyes on the sea."

"It's okay to admit you led us astray."

"Oh, I led us astray, did I?" He shook his head and reached for the horse's reins. "Horse-Ian has to stay here."

She raised an eyebrow at the name. She'd never met anyone like Dell before.

Dell finished tying Horse-Ian to a tree before skimming a hand along the stones. Len followed him until they came upon an opening, barely wide enough to fit through. Dell squeezed himself into it without hesitation. "Come on!"

Helena wedged herself in, the rough rocks scraping her arms as she slid along the narrow gap.

By the time she burst free, her shirt had come untucked and hung down to her knees. Wisps of hair fell wildly about her face.

Her eyes fixed on Dell, his blonde hair unkempt and the bronze skin of his face mottled with bruises. Even so, he was handsome.

Her eyes followed his line of sight as she heard the crash of waves upon the rocky shore.

Pebbles shifted underneath her feet as she made her way to Dell's side.

"Dell," she whispered. "This is…"

"I know."

Sharp crags framed the cove on three sides with the ocean as the fourth.

Helena gazed out at the sun-dappled water as it rose and fell. The faint outline of ships marked the horizon. It was a busy trading zone.

She breathed in, imagining she could see all the way to Bela and the adventure awaiting her there. An adventure of magic and honor she'd never experience.

Instead, council meetings and palace dinners would make up the rest of her life.

"Have you ever thought of leaving?" she asked. "Of boarding one of your family's ships and going to Gaule or Bela or even Dracon?"

"Every day of my life." He sighed and took off toward the water, stumbling as he lowered himself to sit in the black sand beyond the pebbles. He shrugged off the cloak, revealing a torso striped with cuts and bruises. With a groan, he lay back.

Helena ran forward and dropped to her knees at his side. "Dell."

"I'm okay," he grumbled.

"Like hell you are." Helena chewed on her lip. Her mother had taught her many things, but Sophia always demanded she stop at healer duties. A princess shouldn't have to use her hands in such a way. What would Sophia have said if she knew of the knife skills?

"I'm just tired." Dell's eyes slid shut.

"No, Dell Tenyson. Do not fall asleep on me. Wake up, you idiot. What were you thinking riding all the way across the city just to show me the sea? I didn't need to see it. Not when you needed a healer."

A tear tracked down her cheek. What had they done?

"Don't call me that," he muttered.

"What?"

"Dell Tenyson. I'm not one of them."

"Fine. Tell me what I need to do for your wounds."

"Clean… they need cleaned."

He must have meant his cuts. Helena took the discarded cloak and turned to soak it in the water. She held it above Dell to let the water drip into his first gash before wiping it.

A scream escaped his throat, and Helena froze.

"Dell, Dell are you okay. What's wrong?"

"Salt water," he croaked. "Burns."

"Big baby," she muttered, wishing Corban was with them. She didn't understand his healing magic, but she'd seen enough to believe in it.

Dell's voice cut off as he stilled, the only movement coming from his rising and falling chest.

Helena sat back on her heels. "Great." She shook her head and continued cleaning Dell up.

There she was, the princess of Madra, alone, save for an unconscious boy she barely knew, watching the birds fly over the lonely sea. All she could think was how much she didn't want to go back.

Thirteen

Something warm struck Dell's face, waking him from a half-slumber. A bird cawed overhead, but all he heard was the soft laughter coming from nearby.

He breathed in the salty air, lost in the sound.

Wait, salty air? Where was he?

He slid his eyes open slowly, the waning evening sun striking his eyes.

The events of the day came back to him. The Madran games. Fighting Orlo. Len.

He bolted up, hating himself the minute he did as pain ripped through his side.

Len's laughter cut off. "Hey." She approached him with a tentative hand out in front of her. "You should really lie back down."

His eyes found her olive-toned face framed in wild dark curls and his breathing evened.

She bit her fist to muffle another laugh. "I'm sorry. It's just… a bird used your face as a latrine."

The warmth he'd felt before slid down the side of his

cheek. He wiped the back of his hand across his skin. "Ugh, gross."

"I don't know. I thought it rather improved the look."

He shook his head. "Do you make fun of the prince this way?" As soon as they were out, he regretted his words.

Len's expression shut down, ice entering her gaze. "Maybe if you used your brain instead of your fists for one moment, you'd see not all of us fit into the image you have of Madra. Maybe I'm not the woman you think I am." Panic flashed across her face as if she'd said something she shouldn't. "I just mean… don't judge what you don't understand."

She rose and turned her back on him.

Dell leaned on his elbows. He had a habit of saying the wrong thing and pissing people off. But he didn't want to do that with this girl. Mistress of the prince or not, she intrigued him. If she'd tied herself to the Rhodipus', she must have a reason.

Wasn't he tied to them now as well? Thanks to Edmund and Ian, he now had to choose a side. He was either with his family who had never been kind to him, or he was with Edmund who'd been nothing but.

He pushed himself up, ignoring every ache inside and crossing the inky black sand. Len stood with her oversized trousers dragging in the water as she knelt down.

"You're right," he said.

She straightened, raising an eyebrow. "I'm what?"

"You know what I said."

"I do. I just enjoy hearing it is all."

"You frustrate me."

A grin spread slowly across her face and it was as if it lit up the entire world. “Good.”

“Good?”

She nodded. “I sort of destroyed everything for you today. If I didn’t frustrate you, then I’d think you were insane.”

“Why are you still smiling then?”

“Maybe I am insane.”

He finally laughed. “Probably.”

She punched his arm. He flinched, and she covered her mouth. “I’m so sorry. I didn’t even think.”

“S’okay.” He wheezed, his eyes scanning her until he caught a flash of metal in her hand. His brows rose. “Planning to kill me now, are you? And with my own whittling knife? That’s harsh.”

“Whittling… what?” Her eyes flicked to the knife in her hand.

“Whittling knife.” She must have taken it from one of the pockets hidden in his pants. He never went anywhere without it. If the referees had known he had a knife during the fight this morning, he’d have been disqualified. He reached into the other pocket where he always kept his current project. Carving calmed him, but he’d never wanted to share it with anyone before. Len sort of forced it upon him, but he found he didn’t mind.

Her eyes widened when she took in the small wooden angel in his palm. She touched it gently.

“It’s beautiful.”

Pride bloomed in his chest. “My mother taught me.”

“Lady Tenyson can do this?” She picked up the angel, examining every curve.

A harsh laugh vibrated in the air as Dell thought of

his overbearing stepmother doing something so delicate. "No. My mother. We lived in a mountain village when I was younger. I didn't come to the city until she…"

Len set the angel back in his palm and folded his fingers over it. Her eyes met his gaze as his heart thundered against his ribs. Her brow furrowed as if she was trying to figure him out.

"Dell," she whispered his name as a prayer. "I'm trying to figure out how the mottled and bruised fighter I first saw in the streets of Madra can make something so… beautiful."

The edges of his mouth tipped up. "You thought I was a wooden-headed boxer like so many of the highborn lads in this town."

"I don't really know what I thought."

"You know what I think?" The distance between them had somehow vanished.

Her breathy "no" warmed his face.

"We should probably get back to the city before dark."

"Please." Desperation tinged her voice as she pulled away, snapping back to reality at his words. "Just a bit longer."

It struck him then. She didn't want to go back. This wasn't only about what happened at the games. Something in the palace stole the joy from her eyes.

Their moment was forgotten as his jaw tightened. "Are they forcing you to be there? To—"

"No." She touched his hand. "No. Nothing like that. I just… I can't explain it. I want to stay here with you."

He didn't believe her, but what could he do? Storm

the palace and demand the prince fight him? He'd lose, of course. And then where would Len be?

"What did you mean you destroyed everything for me today?" he asked.

Len crossed her arms over her chest and walked up the sandy beach away from him. He followed her to where sand turned to rock.

She reached the base of the cliff and slid down to sit, leaning against the rock wall. Dell joined her.

Her thumbs tapped against each other as she drew her knees in. "You're a Tenyson, Dell. I didn't know that before. But now I see it. And you chose me over your brother."

Dell laughed. "That's what you're worried about? As far as I'm concerned, Ian is nothing to me."

"You absconded with the…" She stopped herself.

His brow furrowed. "With the what?"

She sighed. "With the prince's mistress. That won't be looked upon kindly. I don't think you understand what is probably happening in the city right now. The Madran games have likely shut down early. The palace guard is probably combing the streets. They'll venture out from the city soon. Then they'll travel toward the nearby villages."

None of it made sense. Why would the royal guard search for a mistress? Kings and princes had many. Estevan Rhodipus had never been linked to any before Len, but… the truth smacked him in the face as if a wave rose from the sea to drag him under.

"You're not just a mistress, are you?" It was so obvious now. How could he not have seen it? Estevan had retrieved her from Mari's himself. Not Edmund or some guard, the prince.

Len opened her mouth, but no words came forth as she grappled for truth.

He stood and paced in front of her, each step bringing a new pain, not all of them physical.

Why did he feel so betrayed? He had no right to anything from Len.

She stood, dusting off the butt of her trousers. "Dell, you're right."

He could have made a joke of that as she had, but his mind spun with the new knowledge.

"I'm—"

The words exploded from him. "In love with the prince? Yeah, I figured it out."

"That's…"

He put his hands on his head and breathed through the pain. Then why wasn't she dying to run right back into his arms? No, he hadn't been right at all. He faced her. "No, the prince is in love with you."

A laugh broke free of her. He didn't understand what was so funny.

He gripped her arm, meeting her gaze. "Is he forcing you to stay?" Tradition said Estevan Rhodipus had to marry someone from one of the other five kingdoms. And in Madra, tradition was law. The priests would make sure he adhered to what had always been done.

No matter what he felt, the heir would marry the Gaulean princess.

Len lowered her gaze. "I want to tell you something."

He dropped her arm. "I've heard enough. That bastard is making you stay with him while he marries another. You need not explain anything else. I see it all. The disguises you used to get out of the palace and away from the situation. Your desire to spend more time in the freedom we have without the watchful eye of the prince. If I didn't already hate the Rhodipus line, this would push me farther down that road."

Tears formed in her eyes. "You're against the royal family? All of them?"

He sighed. "The young prince and queen seem okay. But Len, the king and his family have led us into ruin. The people of Madra starve while he plans balls."

"Tradition says the princess has to have a ball to choose a husband before her mask is removed."

"Screw tradition."

She gasped. "You don't mean that. Tradition built Madra into what it is."

"A war-mongering nation? I'm sorry, Len, but Madra is no great kingdom. The king cares nothing for the people and Estevan is no better. The bastard princes are rarely even on Madran soil. We know nothing about the princess. Why is she kept from us? It's not right. She will be head of the merchant council and the merchants are driving the wedge between the classes even deeper. Our freedoms fall down around us and she sits in her palace obeying priests and learning how to take more food from children's mouths to give the merchants."

No tears clouded Len's eyes any longer as they hardened. "Says the merchant's son."

"You know nothing about me." He turned and walked down the beach.

"And you know so much about me?" she yelled at his

back. "I've changed my mind. Take me back to the palace."

"With pleasure."

DARKNESS BLANKETED the world by the time Dell and Len rode back through the city streets.

"Take me to Edmund's," Len said.

They were the first words she'd spoken since they left the beach. The brief moment of peace they'd experienced didn't exist in either of their lives.

"If you take me to the palace, they're likely to arrest you."

He grunted. "I don't need you to explain it to me."

"Sorry."

He scratched the side of his face. "No, it's okay. I'm just…"

"Yeah, me too. Look Dell, I think today was a mistake. We shouldn't have run. Both of us have lives here in Madra that we need to get on with. I don't think I'm going to see you again."

He wanted to tell her different, but he couldn't. She was right. They couldn't seek each other out. But how was he supposed to forget about a girl who made every pain in his life disappear?

A girl whose stubbornness drove him. A girl he…

No. She wasn't his. He had no claim and never would.

They didn't find royal guardsman in the streets but the signs they'd been there were everywhere. Overturned crates, rotten food scattered across the road, horse droppings.

Horse-Ian snorted as Dell tugged on the reins, turning them toward ambassador row.

When they stopped near Edmund's gate, it opened quickly.

A frazzled Edmund froze, his eyes widening. "Len." He rushed forward to help her down from the horse. "We've been searching everywhere for you."

"Edmund." Her voice softened. "I'm okay. I needed to get out of there."

He shook his head. "I don't think you understand how much trouble you're in. The king—"

"Not here, Edmund."

He looked up at Dell as if seeing him for the first time. "Len, get inside. I'm going to have a word with Dell."

She shot him one last apprehensive look before disappearing into his house.

"Dell Tenyson."

Dell had never heard such anger in Edmund's tone. He held his hands in front of his chest. "Look, I'm sorry. I was just helping her get away from Ian."

Edmund swallowed hard, evening his breath. "I know you do not understand what really happened today, so I'm going to explain something to you."

"I know everything," Dell stated.

"No, you don't. Listen to me, Dell. That girl is special. I'm not going to explain how much to you because Madran tradition must even guide a Belaen man inside this city."

"I have no idea what that means."

"Of course you don't. So, here's what will happen: you will forget about Len. You don't know her. Everything you think you know is a lie. You will never see her again."

"You can't—"

"Oh, but I can. This is the bargain you're going to make with me so I don't turn you in to the king for abducting her today."

"I didn't…" Dell narrowed his eyes. "I was trying to protect her."

"If you want to protect her, you will help me keep the Rhodipus in power. You will prevent your family and their allies from throwing Madra into chaos. That is the only thing Len needs from you. She lives in that palace. What do you think happens to her if it's invaded?"

Dell didn't voice the answer he knew in his bones. Rebellion meant death. Any smart rebel leader would want those connected to the king put to death.

Len.

He lifted his eyes to the door she'd disappeared through. She didn't even know the danger she was in. The same feeling that had come to him when the prince showed up at Mari's rushed through his veins, and he knew with a sudden clarity which side he was on.

Not for the king, but for those protected by his power.

He met Edmund's gaze, seeing the same truth in his eyes. Neither of them had a choice. They had to fight for Madra because the alternative was unthinkable.

Fourteen

Edmund stomped back into the house, the door slamming behind him. He didn't stop until he stood in front of Helena. For a moment, they only stared at each other—her in apprehension, him in relief. He closed the short distance and crushed her to him.

"Aw, Edmund," she wheezed. "Were you worried about me?"

"Don't joke about this, Helena. This isn't you escaping the palace to experience the city. You disappeared from the Madran games. Your games. Do you have any idea how upset your father is?"

"I didn't know he cared."

Edmund pulled away from her and held her at arm's length. "Don't be a fool, princess. The king knows you weren't abducted. Quinn has already received his punishment and priests have swarmed the city looking for you."

She batted his arms away and turned to clutch the back of the couch in the sitting area. Quinn. She closed her eyes, releasing a breath. How could she have been so stupid? She hadn't even thought of her brother since leaving the games behind.

"Tell me everything, Edmund." Her voice cracked. "Please."

He seemed to recover from his irritation and he placed a comforting hand on her shoulder. She laid her free hand over his and squeezed.

"Come," he said, his voice gentle as if speaking to a child. "I must return you to the palace. We can talk on the way."

A white carriage waited for them outside his front gate. Helena eyed Edmund. "They knew I'd come here first, didn't they?"

"Stev thought you might."

She flicked her eyes to the royal crest emblazoned on the carriage door. The two wings wrapped around a sword brought another set of wings to mind. The angel Dell carved with such care. Her breath hitched, and she covered it with a cough.

She was the princess of Madra, soon to be head of the merchant council. If anyone knew of the connection she shared with Dell, Tenyson or not, she'd be ruined. If they knew she'd revealed her face to a man, no matter how noble his blood may be…

Another question came to the forefront of her mind. Now that Dell's lineage was known, would he come to the ball? Would he allow himself to be a part of his own family if it meant becoming hers?

No, that was a silly fantasy.

He wouldn't save her from her father choosing Ian for her, or from a life spent wholly within Madra. She'd forever be grateful for today, for the bit of something more he'd shown her.

She only wished Quinn hadn't been caught up in her deceptions.

Edmund hauled himself into the red velvet interior of the carriage and held a hand down to her. As soon as she climbed in and shut the door, they lurched forward, rumbling down the road.

"Father knows I've been in the city without my mask, doesn't he?" she asked.

Edmund nodded, fixing her with a stare. "Quinn had to convince them all you weren't abducted, so he didn't interrogate the Madran citizens."

Helena swallowed. To the king, interrogation was much more than simply asking questions.

Edmund continued. "He showed them the clothing you'd left in the latrine, including the mask."

"What…" She sucked in a breath. "You mentioned Quinn's punishment."

He shifted his eyes to his hands. "He's gone."

"Gone?"

"The king sent him to Gaule."

"But he was supposed to stay until my ball. He was supposed to be there! His assignment to Gaule didn't start until next month."

"Helena." Edmund lowered his voice. "I don't think you understand the gravity of this situation. The priests—"

"Forget the priests."

"I wish." He ran a hand over the top of his head. "I've never understood how Madra could have three sources of power. The king, the merchant council, and the priesthood. Yet, the only one with true power is the priesthood. You've broken one of their longest standing laws. A Madran princess cannot appear as any commoner. She is above them, at least in the priesthood's eyes. You are too sacred to be revealed."

"It's bull."

"It's law."

"Argh!" She slammed her fist into the side of the carriage as it bumped, sending her tumbling sideways.

"Helena—"

"Don't 'Helena' me, Edmund. You're not even from here. I'll bet your Belaen queen never has to deal with such horsescrap."

"No, she just had to deal with a curse that controlled her entire life. Every leader has their own form of shackles."

"I'm not a leader." She leaned back against the wall. "I'm a princess who wears pretty dresses and knows which fork goes with the right dish."

Disappointment flashed across his face. "You underestimate me, Helena. I know you are much more than that."

She met his gaze. How much did he know of her mother's training? All of it, probably. He seemed to know everything.

As if sensing her discomfort with the secrets she carried, Edmund veered away from the subject. "You may never lead an army to war, Len, but I've seen you entrance grown men and women who even I struggle to charm. That has its own kind of power."

"If you're talking about Dell, he just thinks I'm Stev's mistress." She snorted as the reality of that statement hung between them. "What would he do if he knew who I was, and that you were Stev's true mistress?" A laugh bubbled up from her chest.

A wry smile appeared on Edmund's lips.

She calmed her laughter and breathed deeply. "I don't like lying to people. Dell. My father. I don't think I want to do it anymore."

Edmund leaned forward, meeting her gaze. "Then don't." He raised a brow, begging her to challenge him.

Was it really that simple? Tell the truth and people would accept her for it? Or tell the truth and they wouldn't, but at least she tried?

The carriage came to a stop and moments later an unbelievably tall woman in a white priestess' robe yanked the door open.

"We have the princess," she yelled to someone behind her as she reached in and wrapped a strong hand around Helena's arm.

Helena let out a yelp as the priest dragged her from the carriage.

Edmund jumped out after her. "Take your hands off the princess."

The priestess ignored him and turned Helena toward a crowd of others in the same telltale robes.

"Edmund," she called. "Where's Stev?"

"Unhand her." Edmund gripped the large woman's wrist moments before two other priests pried him off and pulled him away.

"What's going on?" Helena yelled, her eyes finding Edmund as she stumbled, her knees hitting the stone before the woman yanked her back up. Another carriage appeared, rumbling through the palace gates.

"I'm going to find Stev," Edmund yelled over the babbling priests who now swarmed her, pushing her toward the carriage.

A tear rushed down her face as the priestess shoved a woven sack over her head threw her into darkness. Someone lifted her. Fear coursed through her veins as her body hit what must have been the bench seat inside the carriage.

Where were her parents? A sob escaped her throat as the carriage jolted forward.

"Shut up, girl," someone hissed. "You brought this on yourself."

Helena bit her lip to prevent more cries from escaping. They had abducted her from her own home.

No, abducted was the wrong word.

The priesthood took her, but she knew they wouldn't do this unless the king allowed it.

This was her punishment.

HELENA HAD HEARD tales of the 'priest hole' like the one they now led her to. The only prison in Madra. The palace didn't cage people, in part because the king didn't want commoners under the same roof as the royal family. He let the priests do the kingdom's dirty work.

They didn't only craft the laws. They enforced them.

But the king could have stopped them if he wanted to. The fact that she was there meant her father wanted it.

She'd betrayed her family and her kingdom, by sneaking into the city without her mask.

Metal rattled as an iron gate swung open and one of

the priests pushed Helena into a darkened hall. Damp air curled around her, sending a shiver down her spine. The musty scent of the stale space had her wrinkling her nose in distaste.

Her tears dried as she prepared herself for what was to come.

Cries came from occupied cells as they passed. Her breath lodged in her throat, and she stumbled. Stiff fingers curled around her arm in a bruising grip, forcing her forward. They pulled the sack from her head and stopped at an empty cell. No special treatment for the princess. She'd be kept in much the same state as anyone else.

An emaciated face appeared at the door of a nearby cell. How long had these people been here? She took in the gaunt eyes and ratty hair.

No, that wouldn't be her.

She didn't know exactly how long they'd keep her, but all of Madra had been invited to her ball at the end of the week. She had to be there, and the priests knew it.

As she stepped into the cell of her own will, she turned and lifted her chin, because she'd realized something else. She narrowed her eyes at the pudgy man locking her in. They couldn't touch her. She was the princess of Madra, and the people must see her unharmed when she finally revealed her face to them.

She sat in the center of her cell and crossed her legs. They could lock her up, but they couldn't take her freedom because she possessed none. They'd just changed her cage from a gilded one to a real one, but a cage was a cage, and she was used to feeling trapped.

They would have nothing from her. And when her

brother became king, and she became head of the merchant council, they'd use their combined power to put the priesthood in their place.

They'd regret the day they made an enemy of Princess Helena Rhodipus.

NOTHING CHANGED IN THE HOLE. Helena didn't know if it was day or if night had descended upon the world. How long had she been there?

They'd fed her mutton stew with watery wine, but how long ago was that?

She leaned back against the wall of her cell, listening to the coughing and wheezing echoing down the long hall. Footsteps sounded against the stone, and she straightened her spine.

Two female priests dragged a thin man past Helena's cell.

She covered her mouth to hide her gasp. A tapestry of blood striped his back. She crawled forward and gripped the bars of her cell.

The woman returned, stopping as soon as they saw her.

"Princess," one of them laughed before kicking the bars of her cell.

She pulled her hands back moments before the boot would have crushed them.

They moved on, and Helena sat back on her heels. Because of that one word, every prisoner in this place now knew who she was.

And it only confirmed what she feared.

Unlike her… they weren't getting out.

PAIN SHOT up Helena's back as she turned onto her side. Sleeping on the stone floor for the last few nights—or what she assumed was night based on when she fell asleep—had wreaked her body.

She pulled her knees into her chest, trying to gather any bit of warmth she could. She wore Quinn's clothes still, which she'd never been more thankful for. Her dress would have been even more uncomfortable.

Quinn. She squeezed her eyes shut, trying not to think of her favorite brother. He was missing her ball, the most important day of her life, because of her selfishness.

His voice wound through her mind. *You deserve some selfishness,* he'd say. He'd always been too understanding for his own good. It was why he'd helped her. He knew how trapped she'd been in the palace. All of them knew.

A tear tracked down her face. Were her brothers ashamed of her? She didn't know what she'd have done locked inside the palace most of her life if it hadn't been for them. Until recently, she hadn't tried to go see the world because they'd brought the world to her.

It was wrong, she realized too late, to be satisfied with that. Traditions or no, she should have always fought for her freedom. Dell made her see that. Stories of the sea and the city were great, but actually experiencing them for herself was life altering.

A key rattled in the rusted lock, and Helena jerked her head up. A wiry older man with thinning gray hair and a manicured beard peered in, his face alight in the glow of the lantern he carried. He offered her a kind smile, the first she'd seen since arriving.

"Princess," he whispered. "I'm glad to see you awake."

She didn't respond.

He took that as a cue to continue. "I'm afraid I have to interrupt your pleasant evening and ask you to come with me."

Pleasant evening? Was this man mocking her?

"My name is Koran." He held a hand down to her.

Helena had made it a point not to learn the names of Madra's priests throughout her life. She'd wanted nothing to do with them, blaming them—rightfully so—for her masked life.

"I won't bite," Koran said, giving his hand a shake. "Please, I promise you want to come with me."

It wasn't like she had a choice. A sigh deflated her chest, and she gripped Koran's hand, letting him pull her to her feet.

The priest tried to hide his disgust at the smell of unwashed bodies as he gently led her to the door, but his nose crinkled.

Helena had grown used to it, sure her own smell wasn't pleasant after so long in her cell.

He found a key on his crowded key ring and unlocked the door. Fresh air struck her the moment she stepped out of the prison.

The monastery that housed the priests was a compound of buildings she'd never visited before. In her studies, she'd learned aside from the prison, they had a winery, as well as lavish living quarters.

The priest led her down a dirt pathway to a nearby brick building. Inside, furnishings were sparse.

Koran released her. "These are my quarters."

Something wasn't right. "Why have you brought me here?"

"Ah, so you do speak."

"Of course she speaks," a third voice said. "Sometimes she won't shut up."

"Stev." As her brother appeared from an adjoining room, she ran toward him, her tired legs faltering.

Stev had never been the hugger of the family—not like the twins—but this time, he wrapped her in his arms as if he never wanted to let go.

"I've been so worried," he said. "We didn't know where you were. Kassander has been crying every night. Cole beat the crap out of a few of father's guards trying to get the information. But you know how loyal they are."

Helena released him and peered up at his tired eyes. "How'd you find me?"

He ran a hand through his hair. "I worried the entire time you might be here, but then I convinced myself father would never allow them to take you. I was wrong. I had Edmund looking into it."

"His spies?" One corner of her mouth quirked up.

Only Edmund would take a post as ambassador in a foreign kingdom and then develop a network of spies better than the ones employed by the prince.

"I reached out to Koran." He sent a nod toward the priest. "I've had him keeping an eye on Kassander's training."

Relief rushed through her at the words Stev wasn't

saying. He didn't trust the priesthood either. "When you're king, Stev…"

"Helena," he said in warning. "We cannot only plan for a future that lays many years down the road. We must deal with things as they stand now. Your ball is tomorrow night. You will return to the palace with me now."

"But father—"

"He cannot punish all of us, can he?"

Her lips quirked up. "Yes, he can."

Stev laughed, the sound so unlike him, Helena stepped back.

His laugh cut off abruptly. "I'm sorry. I'm just so relieved to have you with me."

His face grew serious, and Helena reached up to brush her thumb over his cheek. Her brother tried to hide everything deep inside himself. He always had.

Just as she'd had to hide everything on the outside of her.

"You would defy the king for me?" she asked.

"Of course." His brow crinkled. "You're my sister." He reached into the pocket of his black jacket and procured a simple white mask. "I'm sorry."

"I know." She took it and tied it around her face, finding comfort for once in the feel of the soft fabric.

Koran led them outside into the darkness of the night. Clouds obscured any stars, but a sliver of moon winked in and out of view.

"I couldn't bring a carriage because that would attract attention," Stev explained as Koran retrieved a single horse.

As they rode through the monastery gates and down

the hill into the city, Helena glanced back at the monastery, a shadow looming in the night.

She was delivered from her prison, but what about the others? Why were they there?

Something wasn't right in Madra.

Fifteen

The day of the princess' ball dawned bright in Madra, but quickly turned cold as rain clouds moved across the sky. A storm had churned out at sea for days and finally arrived on their shores.

Dell peered up at the swirling darkness blocking the sun. A torrent of rain erupted from the heavens, crashing down on his head.

Madrans ran through the streets in search of cover, but Dell didn't move.

His sopping clothes stuck to every curve of his body like a second skin and still, his feet remained frozen to the spot.

He had nothing. Not anymore. Maybe he never had—at least not since his mother died.

He hadn't returned to his family's estate after the Madran games where he saved the girl who *assaulted* his brother. Where the world found out he was a Tenyson.

The shopkeepers he'd known for years now treated him as any other merchant—with formality and distrust.

They were always wary of those who brought goods to the kingdom and swindled them.

The night before, he'd slept on the deck of one of his family's ships, but had to leave before the sailors arrived to prepare it to set sail.

The Gaulean ship sat docked in the slip next to it, meaning Princess Camille was still there. A good sign for the royal betrothal, he assumed.

He wouldn't know. His Knowledge of palace happenings was limited. He hadn't even spoken to Edmund since the night he'd returned Len to his home.

Dell shook his head, rain streaming down his face as he finally jogged across the road to an alehouse, showcasing its welcome warmth through the open door.

For once, chatter didn't die down as he entered. Alehouses were the one place people of all stations mixed. Along the far wall, a table of Merchants dressed in their exotic finery bent over a stack of papers between them.

Common folk escaping the deluge outside provided a cacophony of laughter.

A table in the corner was the favored spot of mercenary soldiers. Most people kept their distance from the tattooed men and women who fought for a living. They weren't like those who joined the royal army to feed their families.

Mercenaries spoke as if they enjoyed what they did.

Madran mercenary forces had fought across the sea for the sorcerer they called La Dame until she was defeated. Madran royal forces had been on the other side of that battle. So many families lost their loved ones to war.

The difference was choice. Those in the royal army

had no choice where they were sent or for whom they fought.

Mercenaries chose based on who paid the highest coin.

Where did Dell belong? Even in an alehouse meant to be a meeting place of all people, he didn't fit.

He took the only empty table wedged up beside the mercenaries.

Catsja appeared, mug in hand. "Hi, sweetie." She smiled as she set the ale down. "You look a little lost today." She reached out and trailed a finger down his cheek.

Dell peered up into her dull gray eyes. Catjsa was a beautiful woman with her long, raven hair piled in an intricate design on top of her head. Eyes that spoke of experience with the world. A petite frame.

But he suddenly didn't understand why he'd fought Orlo for her. She was his wife, and Dell was nothing but a potential distraction.

He leaned back, away from her roving hands. "I'm okay, Catjsa." He pulled a coin from his pocket and set it on the table. "Thank you."

She flicked her eyes from the coin to him and back again and shook her head. "No, dear. You're not." She wiped her hands on her apron and glanced behind her to make sure none of the other patrons needed her before sliding into the seat across from him.

"What's on your mind, Dell Tenyson?" She pushed his ale toward him. "It's lunch. Drink up and when you're finished telling me all about this woman you can't stop thinking of, I'll fetch you some bread and cheese."

He met her eyes. "Grapes too… if you have them."

She laughed, and he found he enjoyed her laugh when she lost the predatory glint in her eye. "Grapes too. Now out with it."

He scratched his chin, trying to figure out what he could say without telling her too much. "I have a friend," he began. "And I think she's in trouble."

"How so?" Catjsa leaned forward, listening intently.

"The man she's with… she's alluded to not being allowed to leave."

Darkness crossed Catjsa's face. "That is the way of many marriages."

"But they aren't married. He is to wed someone else. I think she's in danger."

"Then what are you going to do about it?"

"Do?"

"Yes, Dell." She laughed. "If this woman means something to you, there must be something you can do to help her."

Talk from the table beside them froze both Dell and Catjsa.

"Have the rebels contacted us?" one of the mercenaries asked.

"Yes," another affirmed. "And we turned down their offer."

"There have been rumblings," a low voice growled. "Within the royal army itself."

The first snorted. "That's why you never make an oath of infinite fidelity. Then you don't have to break it. They're faithless."

Catsja leaned closer to Dell. "Never thought I'd see the day the royal army turned on the king."

"What's going on?" Dell asked.

"The last few weeks, we've had a lot of mercenaries in here. Seems there are rumors the royal forces may be tiring of the king's wars like the rest of us."

Dell tried to cover his intense interest in the subject by shifting his gaze to the table. "And the mercenaries don't like this?"

"It's the principal. A mercenary is ruthless, but on the rare occasion you get them to give their word, they won't break it. Ever. Killers, but loyal killers at least."

The information took hold in Dell's mind. He needed to talk to Edmund. Did he know of the shifting loyalties of the army? Or the danger it posed for the royal kingdom? The army was the king's power.

"Do you think the mercenaries will join forces with those who wish the king ill?" he asked. As owner of an alehouse, Catjsa knew more of the realm's happenings than most.

"No," she said with conviction. "Mercenaries have rules they live by. One such rule is they don't fight within Madra. They won't support civil war destroying the kingdom."

His shoulders relaxed. That was a relief at least.

Catsja pushed herself up from her chair. "Remember all I've said, Dell. If you care for the woman at all, you will fight for her."

A serving woman arrived with Dell's lunch, but he barely touched it as he drained the rest of his ale and stood.

Catsja was right.

He had to find Len.

And there was only one way into the palace.

He was going to a ball.

AS THE SKIES continued to dump misery down upon the city, Dell ran through the streets. Flashes of lightning lit his way, and thunder rang at his back as if it would rip the world in two. He spotted Agathe in the window of her bakery but ignored her frantic waving to get him to stop. He only had a few hours before the ball.

Only the servants occupied his family's house when he arrived. The great Lady Tenyson was at the docks examining the newest shipment. Was she involved in the coup, or was it his brother's plan? He shook his head. He didn't have any proof Edmund had spoken the truth about his family.

Dell didn't know where his brothers were, but he needed them to stay gone for a while.

He had nothing suitable to wear for a ball, but Reed was about his size. He burst into the dry house, streaking muddy footprints across white tile floors.

One of the maids watched him in disgust, but he couldn't stop to help clean his own mess. Not when he needed to be there for Len. Would they allow her to attend the ball? Who knew the restrictions mistresses faced in the palace? He just needed to see she was ok. Just a glimpse.

Once her safety was plain, he'd fade back into obscurity. Maybe he'd leave the city altogether. He couldn't stay. Not as a Tenyson, both hated by his own family and their enemies, alike.

He thought back to the mercenary units and their strange code of honor. Sure, they'd chosen evil over good time and again, depending on who could pay, but there was an appeal in living life with no care for what one did. In the freedom it allowed. The protection it provided. From disappointment. From the kind of heartbreak he'd known too often in his life.

A door slammed shut somewhere in the house and moments later, Reed appeared in his doorway.

"Dell." He stopped, his eyes scanning Dell from soggy hair to muddy boots. "What are you doing?"

Reed was the least threatening member of the family, but he still followed Ian's every command.

Dell didn't have time to play games with either of his brothers. "I'm going to the ball."

"You…" He glanced back over his shoulder before stepping inside the room and shutting the door. "They won't let you. You have to know that."

Dell turned back to the wardrobe where he found the cloak and mantle he'd been searching for.

He stepped toward the door, and Reed blocked his path. "Not this way, Dell."

"What do you mean 'not this way'? What other way is there for me to leave? Get out of my way."

"Ian and mother are downstairs. If you storm down there, stealing clothes from me as you do, they won't let you out of this house."

Dell met his brother's eye. Reed had never given a care for Dell's wellbeing. Even when they were boys and Dell arrived, mourning his mother and scared, neither brother extended a hand. They'd been nothing but cruel. Yet now, something stirred behind Reed's eyes. Some conflict.

Voices entered the hall. "Our people are in place," Ian's words drifted in to them.

A woman whose voice Dell didn't recognize responded. "And there will be a new king?"

"Yes. With me as head merchant. The Tenysons will stay at the tip of the spiral, never having to worry about the long fall down."

Reed's eyes widened, and he gripped the door handle, ready to tell his older brother of Dell's presence.

Dell whipped his whittling knife from his pocket and lunged for Reed, holding the sharp tip at his throat. "Don't make a sound," Dell whispered.

Ian continued speaking in the hall. "We have been assured all preparations are complete. Our man inside the palace tells me it's time to move. The army stands at the ready."

The woman hummed low in her throat. "I see. My messengers have all departed. Everything will be set. I do wish you extended your trust enough to tell me who will let us in."

Dell strained his ears… waiting.

"I'm sorry," Ian said after a brief moment. "I cannot do that until the time is right."

Their footsteps faded away, and Dell pulled the knife from Reed's throat.

"Dell…" Reed eyed him cautiously. "You could ruin everything."

Dell tilted his head to the side, studying the brother he was only now seeing for the first time. "The question now is—do you want me to ruin everything?"

Reed jerked away from him. "I don't know what you're talking about."

"Those words were treason, Reed." Dell pointed to the door. "Treason! Are you a traitor to Madra?"

"They're trying to save Madra."

Dell laughed harshly. "They're trying to wrest the power from the king, but you can't seriously think they'll use that power to fix the kingdom."

"The king is a worthless fool."

Dell nodded. "And he's cruel and sends too many young men and women to die in senseless battles. But give me a break, Reed. You know Ian. You know the kinds of people he'd associate with." He froze. Edmund was right. His entire family was plotting against the royals.

And he suddenly knew what side he was on.

The side that prevented civil war and didn't allow Ian anywhere near the merchant council's ruling chair.

"I have to go." He pushed Reed out of the way and yanked the door open moments before crashing into Ian.

"Seems we have a problem." Ian's lip curled.

Dell refused to back down. "Seems we do." He prepared for the fight he knew was coming.

Ian put two fingers in his mouth and a shrill whistle sounded. Heavy boots pounded up the steps. Dell didn't know what was going on or why the thugs running toward them were with his brother.

"Lock him in the cellar." Ian gestured toward Dell, and the four men surrounded him, preventing him from escape. One took the clothes he still held and handing them to the wide-eyed Reed.

"You don't want to do this, Reed," Dell called behind him.

Ian laughed. "Of course he does. He's a true Tenyson. Unlike you."

Two of the men wrapped meaty hands around Dell's

arms and lifted him off the ground like he was nothing more than a sack of potatoes.

They marched into the swirling storm, the rain pounding in time with Dell's rapid heartbeats.

"You won't get away with this," he growled as Ian trailed them, wiping water from his face.

"Of course I will. I will soon be one step away from the throne."

One of the men ran forward and unlocked the thin wooden door that led to the cellar. He pulled it open, revealing a staircase down into the earth.

A hand landed on Dell's back, pushing him forward into the door. His feet missed the stairs altogether. He hit the ground with a bone-jarring force, his shoulder slamming into the packed dirt floor.

Ian's face was the last thing he saw before the door slid down, throwing him into complete and utter blackness.

Sixteen

None of them knew. It was one of the first things Helena realized about the servants and advisors who walked the palace grounds. No one told them she was missing or that her own father allowed the priests to imprison her.

If they saw the scene days ago outside the front steps, they wouldn't have recognized her. Except for a few loyal servants allowed into the royal family's wing, they had never seen her face.

So, when she walked by and they bowed with a formal "princess" all she could do was act as if none of it had happened; as if she hadn't lost faith in everything Madra stood for. Laws that resulted in the kind of pain she'd seen in the priests' hole were laws that didn't need to be cemented into the kingdom's sacred traditions. They need to be ripped apart at the seams to find where Madra had gone so very wrong.

When Stev brought her back to the palace the night before, he'd hidden her in Quinn's now empty room.

Cole had hugged her so tight, like he worried she'd disappear again.

And Kassander… her sweet brother refused to leave her side, even sleeping in Quinn's bed with her.

Camille walked at her side as they made their way to the family wing, the soft thumping of her cane now a comforting melody. Because Helena needed a friend. Someone who wasn't simply one of her brothers.

"I'm still surprised my father didn't force you to attend the Madran games." Helena glanced sideways at the foreign princess.

Camille frowned. "I am not of Madra. He cannot command me."

A hesitant smile spread across Helena's face. She'd grown accustomed to and rather fond of Camille's abruptness.

"Are you… are you coming to my ball tonight?" She held her breath, hoping her new friend would stand at her side.

"Now that, dear Helena, I do not have a choice in. It's an important night for you and my betrothal to your brother is to be announced."

Helena's steps faltered. "Are you… okay with everything?"

To Helena's surprise, Camille laughed. "You mean my future husband being in love with Edmund? I have no illusions about love or fairytales. We princesses aren't meant for such things. We secure alliances and consolidate power. We don't fall in love."

A sigh escaped Helena as she pushed open the door leading into the family wing. Camille's words rang true, yet she'd always had an image in her mind of a man sweeping in gallantly and stealing the breath right from her lungs.

She froze as she came face to face with her father for the first time since the Madran games.

Red crept up his neck and a vein stood out in his forehead. Those were the only signs of his distress. The blue and red military uniform he insisted upon wearing was perfectly pressed and his thinning gray hair was combed over the side just like any other day.

"Helena," he barked.

Camille reached out and gripped Helena's hand, letting her know she wasn't going anywhere.

The king advanced. "I sent someone to fetch you from the monastery. He returned only to tell me you were already gone. The priests were quite distraught at your disobedience."

Helena lifted her chin, meeting her father's gaze. "I needed to prepare for my ball, father."

He stepped forward until his shadow loomed over her. "Your insolence is alarming, child. Make no mistake, this ball is but a formality. You will be given a Madran husband of great standing who will not abide by your churlish disposition."

"What will you have them do, your Majesty?" she spat. "I'm already a prisoner within your walls. There is little they can take from me."

The sting spread across her cheek before she realized he'd struck her with the back of his hand. She stumbled back, rubbing her face, as shouting erupted with the arrival of Cole and Stev from their rooms.

Stev ran to her side while Cole used his large frame to force their father back.

"You okay?" Stev asked, bending his head to examine her reddened cheek.

Helena nodded, angry tears burning her eyes.

"Don't touch her," Cole's voice rose above the rest. "You've already destroyed Madra. You sent Quinn away. I won't let you hurt Helena too."

"Let me?" The king growled. "Helena disobeyed a two-hundred-year-old tradition when she revealed her face to the commoners. And then she escaped her punishment."

Stev straightened and turned to their father. "She didn't escape. I had her released."

"You?" The king's eyes shifted between his children. Stev was the heir, the boy who'd always followed his father's every command.

Cole's jaw tightened. "Are we quite finished, father?" He said the last word as a curse.

Helena was the one who answered him. "Yes, Cole. Father and I are very much done. I have a ball to prepare for."

She pulled Camille along with her toward the door to her room. As she shut it behind them, it surprised her to find her mother and Sophia waiting for her.

Chloe Rhodipus rose from her seat to envelop her daughter in a soft hug. "We heard everything," she whispered. "I wish I could have helped you, my sweet girl."

For all the strength and wisdom the queen possessed, she had little power over happenings in the kingdom. But the power to soothe her daughter… that belonged to her wholly.

The tears she'd been holding back flowed freely, soaking into the fur collar of her mother's dress.

Chloe pulled back, untying Helena's mask as she did. "There's my beautiful girl." She smiled. "It looks like you'll have a bruise." Her thumb rubbed gently over where the king had struck. "But nothing your mask and some cream won't cover up. Now, let's prepare you for your night. Madra hasn't seen a princess' ball since…"

"Father's aunt, right?" Helena asked.

Her mother shook her head. "No, my dear. Your father's sister."

"I didn't know he had a sister."

"She disappeared soon after the ball. Some said she was taken by pirates, but most knew the truth."

"What was the truth?"

Her mother sighed, running a hand down Helena's arm. "You cannot keep a princess hidden her entire life and then expect her to suddenly help with the running of the kingdom once you deem her worthy enough to strike the chains from her wrists."

Sophia chose that moment to chime in. "There were no chains on that girl's wrists. I would know. I was her lady's maid before yours."

Helena touched the edge of the mask her mother had laid on the table. "It's a metaphor, Sophia." She smiled sadly. "The mask carries the weight of manacles."

Sophia huffed. "I'm going to go prepare you a bath, princess. When you stop speaking nonsense, come scrub up."

She left and Camille released a breath. "You need a new maid."

Helena shook her head. "Sophia is a stubborn woman, but she's loyal and she loves this family." She dropped into a chair. "I wish tonight was about more than appearances, Mother. The people of Madra think I will choose my husband. But father has already chosen, hasn't he?"

Her mother nodded and reached across the table to grip her hand. "I'm sorry, darling."

Camille crossed her arms over her chest as she sat down. "And here I thought Gaule was a mess with magic folk and non-magic folk at each other's throats. But you people… Madra doesn't even have magic to tear it apart, yet you're just as broken as we are."

"I think every kingdom has its cracks," the queen said.

"Not Bela." Camille leaned forward. "They're so loyal to their queen, it's sickening."

"Didn't she almost die for them or something?" Helena asked. "Father would never even join his men in battle. He thinks the trueborn royals are too valuable. Stev and Kass are forbidden from fighting as well. But I don't see how one man's life means more or less than any other."

The queen stood and kissed the top of Helena's head. "A worthy discussion, but one we don't have time for, I'm afraid."

Camille pushed on her cane for leverage to help her rise. "I'm to seek my own bath. I'll see you soon."

Helena nodded as she left to join Sophia and prepare herself for what should have been the grandest night of her life.

Now she knew it was only another night she'd have to play by the kingdom's rules.

HELENA RAN shaky hands down the bodice of her sky-blue dress. Silver lace created an intricate design around the sapphire jewels sewn on by hand. She twisted her hips to let the flowing skirt swish around her legs.

The looking glass showed her a girl she didn't recognize. Dark hair was piled on top of her head in a mass of curls. Charcoal rimmed her eyes and red coated her lips. She lifted the jeweled silver mask, crafted just for this occasion. As she tied it to her face, only then did she recognize herself.

Who was the princess of Madra without her mask?

Not even Helena knew.

She rose and went to retrieve the glass slippers her father insisted upon. He'd chosen her entire outfit to showcase the wealth of the royal family, even while much of Madra starved.

Only a man would craft glass shoes. They were horribly uncomfortable.

Helena paced the room, trying to get used to the heaviness of her feet, fearing the glass might crack with every step.

She put a hand on her stomach. Breathe in. Breathe out.

It was time.

A knock sounded on her door and Camille poked her head in, her face hidden beneath a mask similar to Helena's.

Helena sucked in a breath. "What are you doing?"

"You're not alone in this, Helena." She smiled, her cheeks pushing against the purple fabric that matched her silky dress to perfection. "Come."

Helena followed her out, taking each step cautiously.

Her brothers awaited her in the sitting room. She breathed deeply to prevent herself from crying and ruining every bit of preparation on her face.

Estevan, Cole, and Kassander each wore masks of their own that kept the top half of their faces hidden from view.

Helena shook her head vigorously. "You don't have to do this." Their gesture was symbolic at best, holding none of the weight her mask held, but it still meant everything to her. "Father is not going to be pleased."

Cole grunted. "I do not live my life to please that man."

Stev stepped forward. "I think what Cole means is we should have done this a long time ago. Until you started going into the city on your own, I never considered how hard this life was for you."

"Come here." She held her arms out and Stev stepped into them. She reached a second arm toward Cole and embraced them both. Kassander wiggled his way in between all of them. "I wish Quinn was here."

"Children," their mother's voice made them break apart. "We must be on our way."

Helena turned to her to find she, too, wore a mask over her delicate features.

Her mother sent her a confident smile and gestured to the door. The six of them filed down the hall with a handful of guards close behind. Servants stared, bewildered as they passed.

The king awaited his family in the room adjoining the ballroom. Music drifted from the party above the sounds of chatter.

Out in the city, Madra may suffer, but in that room, the people were truly alive.

The king scanned his masked family with a scowl on his face. The queen kissed his cheek. "Hello, dear." He turned away from her with disgust and waited for the doors to open.

As they did, the orchestra stopped playing immediately.

A woman dressed in the deep blue livery of the royal family stood to one side as a line of royal guards streamed through the door, stopping abruptly as they cleared a path for the royal family.

The king stepped forward first, and the queen took his arm.

The woman cleared her throat. "The king and queen of Madra."

The cheer that wound its way through the crowd was subdued. Helena scanned the faces with a new realization that the people only did as the king demanded. There was no true love in their desire for favor.

They'd lost faith in him long ago.

And she hadn't seen it. She had once loved her father deeply, and it blinded her to the truth.

But not anymore. Now her trust in him was as broken as the heart beating inside her chest. Irreparable.

As the herald announced her brothers and Camille, she pasted a practiced smile on her face and glided into the great gold-adorned room.

Pillars of cherry wood lined the back wall, stretching up to a ceiling painted to depict Madran victory in battle.

Gauzy white linens wrapped around the pillars giving the room a crisp look. Thousands of candles cast the crowd with an ethereal glow as they waited for her to be announced.

She sucked in a breath and pulled back her shoulders to lengthen her spine. No fear. The week of her name day had consisted of striking the son of the most powerful merchant in Madra, running away to a secluded beach with a boy she couldn't stop thinking about, imprisonment in the monastery, and standing in defiance of her father for the first time.

Compared to the lifetime she'd experienced in the past few days, walking into a ball where many eyes followed her every move was easy.

"Helena Rhodipus, princess of Madra." The herald's voice rang loud and clear.

There was a moment when no sound reached her ears as if the cheers bounced off a protective barrier, allowing her a moment of peace before stepping into the fray.

She lifted her eyes, finding Edmund near the back wall with a wide grin on his face. With a tiny shake of her head, she let him know to drop his magic. She was ready.

As if someone had lifted a veil, noise rushed in, the excitement of the crowd assaulting her.

To the best of their knowledge, their princess stood among them for the very first time. Not on a platform separated from the crowd as at the Madra games or disguised as someone else. For tonight, she was truly one of them.

She tore her eyes from Edmund as Reed Tenyson commanded his attention and lifted her hand to wave as she walked toward the long table where her family now sat, their masks a testament to their love for her.

The king left them to speak with a gaggle of merchants vying for his attention.

As Helena sank into her seat beside Estevan, she sighed. "I'm already exhausted and we only just arrived."

Cole laughed from his spot on her other side. "Do not worry, sister. Soon, all eyes will be on me anyway."

"It's good to know that the center of attention at my ball will be my brother." She shook her head.

He flashed her a grin.

Camille, as the only person not of Madran royalty at their table, leaned forward. "We have balls in Gaule, but nothing so grand as this."

The music began anew, sending soft notes drifting on the air.

Helena opened her mouth to respond, but was cut off as her father appeared with Lord Nirol, a man who spent his life trying to climb the spiral by any means necessary. He was a merchant, but rumors also circulated about his piracy. Helena had met him many times before when the merchant council met with the king at the palace.

Each time had been more unpleasant than the one before it.

"Daughter," her father began. "You will dance." He nodded to Lord Nirol.

"Princess." Lord Nirol dipped his balding head and offered her one bony hand.

With no other choice before her, she ripped her eyes from her father and stood, taking the lord's hand.

He gave her a watery sideways smile as he led her onto the crowded dance floor and placed a hand on her waist.

This was what she'd been training for her entire life.

The dance lessons. Etiquette classes. Helena was bred to be the perfect princess, the perfect hostess. For this night. The night when grown men twice her age would fight for her hand in marriage, some for their sons and some for themselves.

She searched her mind for something to say.

"Did you enjoy the games?" Lord Nirol asked.

She followed his lead in the dance, never once taking it from him—just as she'd been taught. Let the man lead in all things. It was what a princess did.

And it was utter bull.

Helena bit back everything she wished she could say and nodded demurely. "I enjoyed them very much."

It was the only acceptable answer. A Madran princess couldn't admit she found boxing rather barbaric. She'd seen what damage it had done to Dell—multiple times. But the sport was as sacred as anything in their kingdom. She much preferred watching swordplay or practicing with her knives.

Lord Nirol smiled, his yellowed teeth crooked. "I did quite well in my own match."

She couldn't remember seeing him fight before leaving the arena, but he was quite small. Something Stev once told her flashed in her mind. *A merchant speaks truth when it suits him and lies when it gets him what he wants.* What did a merchant want? She'd been naïve enough to ask. *Power.*

So, she'd give him the perceived power he sought. "I saw your match." She smiled. "You impressed me, my lord."

Desire sparked in his narrow eyes. He thought he could gain the power he wanted through her.

"It is a shame you had to leave the games early." He leaned in closer, hoping for the truth of that night. The king's guards had combed the city, but never told the people their princess was missing. They'd been told she retired early to conserve her energy for the ball.

Lord Nirol didn't seem to believe that, but she didn't answer his questioning gaze. As the music rose to a crescendo, vibrating across her skin, she scanned the waiting crowd, many of whom wanted the very thing Lord Nirol assumed he would soon have.

But Helena had been hidden away her entire life. The people didn't know her at all. Tonight, every bit of the kingdom's power rested in her. No matter the ploys her father attempted, in the end, the choice of a husband who would enlarge the Rhodipus grip on Madra was supposed to be hers.

And she wasn't going to give up her power. Not to Lord Nirol. Not to any of them.

Especially not to her father.

Seventeen

A thin stream of moonlight flitted across the dirt floor of the cellar as it broke through a crack in the wooden door.

Dell gripped the leg of the broken chair he'd found among the barrels of root vegetables and casks of wine.

He stood on one of the rickety steps leading up to the door and slammed the wood into the rusty lock over and over.

Nothing.

He grunted as he pounded on the door and released a howl of frustration.

His brother couldn't do this to him.

He jumped from the staircase to search for something to ram into the wood hoping to break the door since the steel lock wouldn't budge.

He gripped the edges of a wine cask, rocking it back and forth to slide it across the floor to access the space behind it where he knew a few tools were kept.

Dell couldn't remember the last time he'd had reason to enter the cellar.

His stepmother's men who were a constant presence at the estate came and went regularly with loads from the ships that came in.

Dell had long known there'd be no reason to keep legal merchandise hidden below the house. Most of his father's goods were transferred from the ship to a warehouse near the docks before being delivered to shop keepers or sent on to one of the other kingdoms.

But the items in the cellar were… different. He wondered if his family only wanted to avoid import fees or was there something else? Most of their goods were kept in warehouses by the docks, not their personal residence.

The wine was easy to explain. It was for the family's consumption.

Other than the wine, bolts of silk, pounds of fine sugar, and a few other items took up the space.

But there was no time to consider all his brothers' illegal activities when only one truly mattered: treason.

Dell had to get to Edmund and soon.

He felt his way along the barrels until he reached the other side where an open bucket held tools. Wrapping his fingers around the first one he saw, he pulled it free.

A shovel with a dirt-crusted iron head. He climbed the stairs once again and stuck the sharp end of the shovel into the crack running the length of the door.

Wrenching on the shovel, he put all his strength into it.

It wasn't enough. He needed more leverage. Shifting his feet so all but his toes hung off the step, he yanked down with such force it pushed him back. His feet tilted and he barely had time to think before he fell back. The shovel clattered to the ground seconds before Dell slammed into one of the barrels on his way down.

The lid of the barrel had only been resting on top and it popped free, jolting Dell as it crashed onto his head.

He groaned and rolled onto his side. "Bloody brilliant." A harsh laugh escaped him and echoed across the dark room. He winced as he rose onto his knees, using the now open barrel to pull himself up. He placed a hand on each lip of the barrel and closed his eyes, willing the pain to fade from his body.

The sliver of moonlight struck the cask in front of him as he opened his eyes, revealing a black substance.

Curious, he stuck his hand inside, pulling up a handful of fine black powder, not unlike the sand from the beach he'd taken Helena too.

But this was no sand.

His eyes widened as he dug his hand in again, his fall a distant memory.

He eyed the row of barrels as if they would explode right where they sat, but he had to know. Picking up the shovel, he moved to the next one and pried the round wooden lid free. He barely heard it hit the ground as his mind filled with what was before him.

The same powdery substance.

Six barrels, all the same.

He stumbled back, rubbing the crown of his head.

What was his family doing with six barrels of explosive powder? They could take down the entire palace wall and a part of the city with it. Was that the plan?

And Dell couldn't do a thing when he was stuck in the bloody cellar.

He yelled, knowing full well no one would hear him.

He'd been unsure which side was truly noble in this fight, but now he had no confusion.

His family had to be stopped.

He launched himself up the steps and smashed his fists into the door, feeling slightly less useless for at least trying.

Desperation raced through his mind. Was it too late to stop the rebellion? Had everything already been set into motion?

He hit the cracked wood until blood ran between his knuckles and pain reverberated up his arms.

He moved down the stairs and sat with his back leaning against the deadly barrels. His brother had taken his whittling knife, the one thing that always kept him from losing his mind.

He patted the pocket where it usually lay.

The one thing Ian hadn't taken was the half-carved piece of wood that made up his newest project. He fingered the rough edges, not yet sanded smooth.

Even after Edmund told him he could never again see Len, he started this… for her.

It was going to be the most perfect thing he'd ever made. A pair of beautiful shoes, meant for dancing, but also running away.

With these shoes, he'd wanted to tell Len she could be anyone she wanted to be. She could run away from the palace. She could run toward it. Her life was her own. The only thing that decided her fate was the direction she pointed her shoes in.

Freedom. Such a simple thought, yet so complicated for them both.

The shoes weren't complete. He'd only carved the

shape of one and had yet to add any embellishments to give it the beauty Len deserved.

Who was he kidding? She'd probably never receive it. He was now a prisoner more than ever before. Would they ever let him go?

And Len… if he couldn't save her, she'd have her fate rest with that of the royal family's and he didn't like their odds.

He tucked the half-carved wood back into his pocket where it lay heavy against his heart, an idea as hopeless as his current state.

With a sigh, he rested his head back against the rounded surface of the barrel and let his eyes slide shut—not out of exhaustion, but only the weariness of failure.

A thud sounded against the door and his eyes snapped open.

The lock rattled, the sound of scraping metal ringing loud in his ears, filling his mind with one thought. Escape.

Were his brothers already returned from the ball? How long had it been? They'd come back to torture him with their cruelty. Or had they come to retrieve their powder?

The door swung open and a wide-shouldered man peered in, the moonlight casting him in a glow. Tattoos snaked up his thick neck, stopping below a square jaw.

His lips set in a grim line.

Dell waited, refusing to shift his eyes away from the man. If this was Ian's punishment, he'd take it. And then one day, he'd get his revenge.

"Dell Tenyson?" the man asked, his voice a low rumble.

"Let's get this over with." Dell narrowed his eyes. "Do what you came here to do."

The man descended the stairs slowly, stopping in front of Dell. His tattoos were more visible now, marking him as mercenary. Even his brother wouldn't seek a mercenary. If they didn't take the job you offered, they were notorious for the harsh treatment they'd give those who sought them in the mountains.

Ian may plan treason against the king, but that couldn't be mistaken for bravery. He was a true weasel.

Another face appeared at the door above, and it took Dell a moment before relief crashed into him.

"Mari?" he asked, flicking his eyes from her to the imposing man in front of him.

"Dell, dear." She shook her head. "Look at the trouble you've gotten yourself in now. Come on now… we have to go."

Dell scanned the cellar with its exploding contraband one last time before following the mercenary up the steps.

Corban waited for them outside. He didn't say a word as he immediately took Dell's hand.

Warmth flooded Dell and every ache that had been present since his fight at the Madran games dulled until they no longer existed at all.

Mari nodded. "Now that we have that taken care of, Dell, this is Toren. Edmund has him protecting us." She gestured to the big man.

He shouldn't have been surprised Edmund had mercenaries in his employ. "Why do you need protection? Has something happened to you?"

"Edmund is worried we will be sought out should

there be a shift in power here in Madra. We are to take a ship to Bela. And you are to join us."

Dell shook his head. "I can't leave."

"Dell, Madra is no longer safe for you. Edmund has learned some concrete things about your family, proving what he suspected to be right."

Who'd told him? Dell only just heard everything Edmund had wanted to know. He froze. "Who told Edmund I was locked up?"

"I don't know, but we must be gone from here now."

"Mari." Dell grabbed her wrist. "I can't. You don't understand. It's so much worse than Edmund feared. There are barrels of explosive powder down there." He pointed to the cellar. "Enough to bring down the sector of the city around the palace walls."

She exchanged an alarmed look with Toren. "Edmund must be told."

"I have to get to that ball."

Mari considered him. "If you appear at the ball looking like yourself, your brother will do more than lock you in the cellar. No, we can't have Dell Tenyson show up at the palace."

"I don't have a choice, Mari."

"I know you don't. Follow me." She turned on her heel and put a hand on Corban's shoulder to lead him across the soggy ground to the barn. A pool of standing water blocked the barn doors, but Mari crashed through it, not caring about soaking her shoes. Toren pulled open the barn door.

The cow mooed as soon as they were all through. Horse-Ian's stall stood empty, as he'd been used along with another horse to pull the Tenyson's carriage.

The mules and goats roused themselves, sticking their heads over the metal bars of their pen.

Mari scanned the space, taking in every unimportant detail before rounding on Dell. "First, if you are to be comfortable, you need dry clothes. It doesn't matter what you put on. We'll wait."

Dell, not wanting to argue when she seemed as if she had a plan, walked to his bunk and exchanged his still-damp clothing for dry wool trousers and a linen shirt.

Mari nodded in approval. "You're not going to feel anything," she promised.

She lifted her hand and curled her fingers. Dell would never get used to her magic. She'd used it on him before, and he was always suspicious if it worked as well as she claimed it did.

As he glanced down at his clothing, he didn't notice a difference.

Toren's eyes widened.

"What? What do I look like?" Dell asked.

Corban circled him, his eyes appraising.

Mari was the one who answered. "Dark hair slicked back into a perfectly groomed tail. A handsome, yet open face with wide amber eyes and a strong jaw. Clothing fit for a prince. Blue pants, a white ruffled shirt, and a pale blue jacket. Shoes shined to perfection." She smiled. "One of my better creations, I'd say." She turned toward the door. "Come."

At the side of the barn sat a rusty mule cart. The air around the cart grew hazy, shimmering as if tiny waves rippled the air.

When it cleared once again, the cart had been replaced by a large white carriage with gold rimming the door. For as many times as Dell had been the subject of Mari's magic, he'd never witnessed his own perception changing.

Taron led the two mules from the barn. Mari faced them and they transformed into massive black steeds with shining coats and jewel-encrusted bridles.

Mari smiled in satisfaction as Dell reeled back. "No one at the ball will know who you are, Dell. Being a mystery carries its own set of dangers. My magic will only last for about two hours. You must get in, inform Edmund of everything you've seen, and then get to the ship in slip fourteen. We leave for Bela on the morning tide."

Dell reached forward to stroke the soft nose of the massive beast, the weight of what he was being asked to do sat heavily on his mind. There'd been a time when the only life he expected for himself was that of a simple farmer in his mountain village.

But everything changed in an instant, and now he found himself with the fate of a kingdom on his shoulders.

Dell. Not a Tenyson by any other meaning than birth. A lowborn kid.

Now he had to save a king who didn't deserve to be saved in order to protect the ones who did.

He nodded slowly and released a breath. "I'll be there, Mari."

Eighteen

Large torches lined the entryway, past the wide-open gates. No one in Madra would be turned away tonight. Even the commoners were allowed entry into the ball. Some would arrive for the sheer novelty of the event. Others had the delusion in their mind they had a chance to be chosen as the princess' husband.

Dell knew how it truly worked. The king would choose someone whose power enlarged his own.

Ian.

He was the best choice to make a connection between king and the merchant council. Dell knew it. Everyone knew it.

But Ian would be the end of the Rhodipus line.

Dell's carriage rumbled to a stop, and he swallowed past the lump in his throat. His eyes flicked down over his plain clothes and he tried to see what they would see. To him, he still looked like Dell—the Tenyson boy who was kept in the stables as if he were an animal himself.

His breath quickened as the door opened and a white-gloved man in doublet and tails bowed. "Welcome to the palace, my lord."

Dell hesitated for a moment, glancing around at the opulence of his carriage. They didn't know who he was, but they could see he was important.

A foreign lord? Maybe they'd assumed he came from Gaule or Cana to attend the grand event. He lifted his chin as he'd seen his brother do a million times before. "Are you going to help me out of this carriage or stand there gawking?" His voice sounded false to his ears, but the servant snapped to attention and extended his hand.

"Yes, sir. Sorry, sir."

Dell took the hand and descended the steps. Another carriage pulled up behind his, and he spared it barely a glance.

The grounds swarmed with servants and guards. As he looked into the man's face, it struck him how young he was. He must have been even younger than Dell himself.

Dell released him and the boy's cheeks flushed. "Sir, do you need an escort into the ball?"

Dell scoffed. "Young man, I have been to this palace more times than you've celebrated your birth."

It was a bold lie. Dell would have benefited from the escort, but he passed the servant without another glance as Toren—disguised as the carriage driver—snapped the reins and left to join the lines of others.

A steady stream of people, nobles and commoners alike, made their way through the palace and Dell followed the flow.

The ball had a strict dress code, so only commoners who could afford the levee dress coats were present. Shop keepers. Ship captains. Wine makers.

Dell, even as the son of a merchant, felt out of place.

Massive carved oak doors stood open, revealing the elegant ballroom packed from end to end. In the center, couples glided across the floor, dancing to the lively orchestra music.

The crowd parted as the princess took her place among them, standing opposite Ian. Dell had only ever seen her up close once when they met at the docks, but she'd barely spoken.

A jeweled mask covered everything she must have been feeling as every eye followed her. Ian pulled her close and her lips, the only visible part of her face, tugged down.

He leaned in to whisper into her ear, and her jaw clenched.

Dell couldn't take his eyes from them even as a servant walked by carrying a tray of wine glasses.

"My lord."

The words echoed vaguely in his mind.

"My lord." The servant stopped in front of him, her eyes tilting with concern. "Are you okay, my lord?"

She'd been talking to him? The title of lord didn't sit well with him. But what could he say? *I am no lord.* His cover would be blown. Mari's magic made them all see something new, but he still felt like himself.

He rubbed a hand over his jaw and took a glass from her tray. "I'm fine." He drained the wine without coming up for air and handed the empty cup to her.

He found Edmund standing near the far wall with Reed by his side. Without another glance at the servant who still stood in front of him, he marched across the room, barely seeing those who had to move out of his way.

Edmund's brow furrowed in confusion as Dell stopped right in front of him. "I need to speak with you," Dell said, his eyes flicking to his brother who now watched him curiously.

"I'm sorry." Edmund leaned forward to look more closely. "Do I know you?"

"Edmund." Dell blew out a frustrated breath. "You told me to put my faith in you. That having something to fight for changed your life. I now know what you meant."

Edmund's eyes widened in understanding. "Excuse me, Reed. Lord… Isaacs is an old friend I did not recognize at first. I must speak with him."

"Of course." Reed glanced from Edmund to Dell and back again. "Remember what we've spoken of."

"I will."

Reed nodded and disappeared into the crowd.

All sound abruptly ceased and Dell jumped. "Dammit, Edmund, I will never get used to that."

Edmund's voice was low as he spoke. "I sent Mari and Taron to get you out of Madra. When Reed told me what you'd overheard…" He shook his head. "We're lucky Ian didn't kill you outright."

"Since when is Reed on our side?"

"Since he learned who Ian is working with inside the palace."

"Who is it?" Dell asked.

"He hasn't told me yet." Edmund glanced over his shoulder at the crowd whose sounds couldn't reach them while his magic was at play. "Reed doesn't trust me. But he didn't want Ian to kill you."

Dell wished it didn't surprise him that someone in his family wanted him to live.

Edmund reached out to grip Dell's arm tightly. "Mari's magic is dangerous, Dell. It fades and you won't be able to feel it happening. You shouldn't have come."

"I know."

"We have people in place for when the rebellion begins. There is nothing more you can do Dell. It's because of you Reed told us our most crucial piece of information. There is someone very close to the royal family making a power play. Now it's time to consider your own safety."

"I can't!" The words burst out of him. He clamped his lips shut and looked to the people on the nearby dance floor. They still couldn't hear him. "Edmund, listen to me. My brother… they have half a dozen barrels of explosive powder."

Edmund's grip on his arm tightened. "Are you sure?"

"I know what it looks like, Edmund. Where would they get it?"

"The mines of Dracon." He sighed and pried his hand free of Dell's arm.

"That's why whoever is planning this needed my brothers. There's no way that much explosive powder could get through the ports of Bela or Gaule. Tenyson ships must have been going into Dracon in secret."

Edmund's eyes scanned the room. "I need to go deal with this, Dell. We must prepare. This changes nothing for you. If you're found in Madra by someone connected to this rebellion, they'll kill you. Get to the ship. I'm going to send Camille to you once the ball ends and I can get her out of the palace. When you arrive in Bela, tell them you must speak with the king or queen. They will protect you should Madra be taken over."

"What about you? Edmund, this isn't even your kingdom. You need to come with me."

Edmund shook his head, his eyes drifting to the table where the crown prince sat masked beside his future bride. "There are reasons…" He met Dell's eyes. "I grew up in Gaule. Bela is my home. But my heart resides here, and I will protect him with everything I have." His eyes widened, realizing what he'd just revealed.

Dell took a step back. It all made sense now. Why Edmund would fight for a king such as the one they had. Why he had so much faith in the prince.

Edmund was in love with Estevan Rhodipus.

And that love was going to kill him because they couldn't win. Not against a mostly unknown enemy who had such tools at their disposal. Not when the king they protected wasn't beloved by the people. Who would fight for him?

Edmund would fight for Stev.

Dell was leaving.

They'd already lost.

The princess drifted by, still in the arms of Ian. Everything about her was stiff, but there was something so familiar in the way she held her head high as if nothing in the world could hurt her. Not Ian. Not the mask she had to wear.

"You need to go now, Dell." Edmund gripped his shoulder. "Before the magic wears off."

"Release your magic, Edmund. There's music playing." He shrugged off Edmund's hand. "I'll leave, but not until I save a princess from a beast."

Chatter crashed in at them, rising above the music, assaulting his every sense as Edmund's magic faded away.

"Dell." One warning. That was all Edmund gave him before Dell made his way toward his brother, holding a beauty captive.

He had to ruin one final thing for Ian. If tomorrow saw the end of this family's rule, this girl wouldn't spend another minute trapped in Ian's embrace.

The music stopped and dancers turned to clap. Dell stepped up to the princess' side and bowed. "Princess," he said smoothly, a smile playing on his lips. "Would you do the honor of giving me the next dance?"

Ian growled. "I don't even know who you are, but the princess and I are not finished." He clamped a hand on the princess' bare shoulder.

Dell lifted Ian's hand off the girl who still hadn't spoken. "I believe she can choose a partner for herself."

A smile formed on her lips, and she hid it behind a cough before extending one delicate gloved hand to Dell.

He took it and led her away from his seething brother.

The Dell of weeks ago never would have imagined sharing a dance with the mysterious princess who was kept behind the high palace walls. Yet there he was, sliding his hand around her waist.

She still hadn't said a word, but he smiled kindly at her. What had Edmund called him? "It's a pleasure to meet you, Princess. I'm Andrew Isaacs."

She gazed up at him, her eyes two deep green orbs in the holes of the mask. What did she look like below that lacy fabric? He imagined she'd take his breath away.

As he stared into her entrancing eyes, something familiar struck him. The music began, and he shook it off as the dance began. He couldn't remember the last time he'd danced, but the moves his mother taught him as a boy came back naturally.

The princess coughed lightly, clearing her throat. "Thank you."

Her voice was so quiet he almost didn't hear her. "For what, Princess?"

She didn't respond.

He couldn't help the next question that left his mouth. "What did Ian say to you?"

She widened her eyes in surprise but only gave a slight shake of her head.

Dell pulled her closer. "I saw the way you tensed when he spoke to you."

"How do you know it was because of him and not the dancing?"

He flattened his fingers against her spine, forgetting for a moment just who she was. He may not understand a lot of things, but women always made sense to him. It had gotten him into more trouble than he could remember.

He leaned close, speaking into her ear. "Because when I move, you follow. No fight. No tension. Your body is relaxed in my hands. You don't know me, Princess. Do I make you feel safe?"

A beat of silence passed between them before soft peals of laughter vibrated from her throat.

He knew that sound.

But it wasn't until she spoke again it struck him. "Do those lines work with the ladies of the city, my lord?"

Len.

He stumbled away from her. His Len… the girl he'd

do anything to see again… she was the princess of Madra.

How did he not see it? The boy's clothing. Escaping the palace.

Helena. Princess of Madra.

My heart resides here and I will protect him with everything I have.

He knew why Edmund was doing it now. For them. Had he known? Of course he did. Len wasn't the prince's mistress. She was his sister. And she was in danger.

"Lord Isaacs," she asked, her lips tilting down. "Is everything okay?"

He glanced toward the door where he knew he should go at that very moment. There was a ship waiting for him. A way to safety. To a new life.

His eyes returned to the princess who looked to him with such innocence. Such beauty. He was one of the few people who knew what lay beneath the mask. Was he the only one who knew what lay inside her chest?

Or had Len been a lie?

Who was the girl in front of him?

He reached out, trailing a finger over the side of her mask.

"Would you like to walk in the gardens?" she asked. "I think I need a bit of air."

The gardens were in the opposite direction of the palace gates. Farther from his freedom.

He nodded, unable to stop himself. "Yes, Princess. Yes."

Nineteen

Ian's gaze burned into Helena's back as she slid her arm into the unknown noble's beside her. She couldn't claim to know many of the wealthy people of Madra since she spent her life cooped up in the palace. But there was something about him… His smile oozed with charm and with his handsome face, she was sure he had the ladies of Madra chasing after him.

His tailcoat with gold buttons spoke of wealth.

But unlike Ian Tenyson, his eyes were not those of a predator. They held something… kinder.

She spied her father speaking to a few of his advisors, paying no attention to her. Stev's eyes followed her, but he didn't rise. He'd have a few guards trail them in the gardens, no doubt.

As soon as she stepped through the door to the gardens, the cool night air struck her and she smiled. Out here, there wasn't an entire host of nobles and commoners expecting bits of her time. There weren't expectations or traditions.

She wished she could strip the mask from her face.

But she had to remember she didn't walk alone.

A shiver raced down her spine.

"Are you cold?" Lord Isaacs asked.

She shook her head, not wanting to return to the ball. Slipping her arm from his, she continued down the path, wishing she could take off the shoes they'd forced her into and run.

She'd run away from everything. Just as she had before… with Dell. Her mind drifted to him, wondering what he was doing. Had he forgotten about her?

Her foot struck a rock on the trail and she cursed as a crack rent the air.

"What was that?" Lord Isaacs asked.

Helena sighed and lifted the hem of her dress. "They made me wear slippers made of glass." She slipped off her shoes and picked them up to examine the broken toe. "Can you believe it? Glass? As if that isn't the stupidest idea you've ever heard."

Lord Isaacs leaned forward to look at the shoe, his dark hair falling into his eyes. He laughed. "Maybe they wanted to make sure you couldn't run away."

She'd had the same thought. A laugh bubbled out of her. "I don't know, but they'd be good if I needed to incapacitate a certain merchant's son." She clapped a hand over her mouth. "Oh my, I can't believe I just said that." Heat rose in her cheeks. "You're going to return home and tell everyone of your walk with the completely insane princess who is a danger to all men and their uh… sensitive parts." She stepped back. "Oh wow… shut up, Helena."

Lord Isaac grinned as if she was the most entertaining thing he'd ever seen. "Not only that, but she apparently talks to herself."

She buried her face in her hands. "I never speak like this. Normally, no one ever knows what I'm thinking. I don't know why everything is spilling out like some weird kind of word vomit—Oh my, Helena, don't say vomit. That is not attractive." She lifted her face. "Not like you even know if I'm attractive—or care—I'm a princess. I don't have to be pretty." She turned away from him. "I'm going to go crawl in a hole now."

Lord Isaacs grabbed her arm before she could walk away. "It doesn't matter what's underneath the mask."

She turned to face him, her brows drawing together.

He lifted a finger to run along the bottom of her mask and she sucked in a breath.

"And not because you're a princess." He stepped closer to her.

She barely knew this man, but his words paralyzed her. She released a soft breath. "Then why?" She met his swirling gaze, trying to see what was behind the intense eyes. "What do you see?"

"Everything," he whispered. "You're beautiful."

His lips crashed into hers and he pulled her against his lithe frame. She returned his kiss, no longer caring she'd only just met the man. Something about him spoke to her, told her to trust him. And she felt seen for the first time in her life.

Not the princess.

Not the girl dressing in her brother's clothes.

Her.

Helena.

She pulled away, breathing heavily, and rested her forehead against his. "Who are you, Andrew Isaacs?"

He pushed her back and seemed to gather himself. "I'm someone who shouldn't be here."

She didn't take her eyes from his and as a flicker of light from the nearby torch passed over them, she would have sworn they shifted, becoming rounder and losing the angular tilt.

She knew those eyes but from where?

He took a step back from her scrutinizing gaze.

"What's happening?" she asked. "Your eyes… they changed."

He snapped his head up. "I have to go." He turned to stalk across the garden.

"Wait." She ran after him, her short legs struggling to catch up with his long strides.

"I can't be here." He sped up, yanking open the door as they passed the guards Stev had sent after them.

The commotion at the door caught the attention of more than a few onlookers, but Lord Isaacs didn't pause.

"Helena," her father scolded, appearing at her side as she marched through the crowd. "Why on earth are you carrying your shoes?"

"They're glass, father," she said, shoving the shoes into his chest. "Figure it out."

Lord Isaacs reached the hall, and she chased after him, not catching up until he stood at the top of the stairs leading down to the carriages.

"Please." She hated the pleading sound of her voice. "Tell me what's going on."

Lord Isaacs finally turned to her, but his dark hair had

turned into a light brown and grew lighter still. "They're coming for you, Princess. Keep yourself safe. Trust only Edmund."

What did he know of Edmund?

"Who are you?" she asked. "Are you threatening me?"

How had she gone so wrong in trusting his sweet smile?

"No." He ran a hand through his now blonde hair. "God, no. If something happened to you…" He glanced to where his carriage appeared, pulled by a horse she would have sworn was shrinking as she watched it.

He reached into an inside pocket of his jacket and pulled something free before pressing it into her hand.

"I wish I could give you the freedom you wanted, Len. But I'm going to do everything in my power to protect you. I promise you that." As if losing a battle within himself, he lurched forward, his hands cupping her face gently as he kissed her confused frown.

He pulled away too soon, sparing her one final glance before sprinting down the stairs and jumping into the carriage. The driver snapped the reins as hard as he could and dust kicked up around the wheels as he left her stunned on the step.

She touched her lips with her free hand and opened the fingers of her other. A rough carving of a wooden shoe sat in her palm, half-finished.

"Dell," she breathed.

There was no other explanation. She didn't understand why he'd been there or how he hadn't looked like himself, but his warning rang clear in her mind.

I'm going to do everything in my power to protect you. I promise you that.

What did she need protected from?

Only trust Edmund. She turned on her heel. The Belaen ambassador had a lot of explaining to do, beginning with —who was Dell Tenyson and what did he have to do with impending trouble in Madra?

Twenty

The carriage shook and quivered around Dell as it raced through the streets. The roof shimmered, winking in and out of view before disappearing entirely. The walls shrank, retracting until they were nothing more than cracked wooden beams rising knee-height.

Dell shook his head, trying to wrap his mind around what was happening as his heart hammered in his chest.

"The carriage…"

They slowed to a stop as Taron pulled into an empty alleyway.

"It disappeared," Dell stammered.

Taron twisted around on the bench he sat on to look at Dell. "It was never there to begin with." He dropped the reins and jumped from the bench, landing beside the mule who'd appeared as a giant horse only moments before.

How did one get used to magic?

Most people in Madra lived their entire lives never

witnessing the power. Maybe it was easier that way. Seeing what magic-folk could do… it changed everything.

Dell climbed from the bed of the rickety mule cart. It was nothing more than rotting wood and rusting wheels now.

He brushed a hand over his face. "Do I look like myself?"

A shadow appeared at the end of the alley.

Taron grunted. "Everything now appears as it should. Time to go. You won't be safe until you are aboard the ship. We leave in a few hours, once Edmund brings the Gaulean princess to us."

Dell took a step back, Helena's face firmly in his mind. But it wasn't the masked face of the princess. He saw Len, the woman who'd befriended him, cared for him. The girl with dark hair, wild from tangling in the ocean breeze, whose frame disappeared among her brother's clothes.

That girl was no princess.

But Len wasn't real. Helena was.

And he still couldn't leave her.

"I'm not coming with you." He lifted his eyes to regard the big man stubbornly.

"Don't be a fool, boy. The only thing left for you in Madra is death."

Dell advanced on him. "And what of the royal family? Is death the only thing here for them as well?"

"That is no longer your concern. Edmund has left orders to bring you with us."

"It's a good thing Edmund is not my keeper then, isn't it?" He narrowed his eyes. "I won't leave when they're in danger. When she's…"

Understanding dawned in Taron's eyes. "You fight for someone other than yourself?"

"I do."

"That is a… foreign concept to mercenaries, but it is what we all wish for. Something to bring us hope. Mari is going to have my head, but I will not force you to come with us, Dell Tenyson." He turned and grabbed the mule's harness, unlatching him from the cart. "I do not think you will survive this, but I wish you luck."

He met Dell's gaze over his shoulder and nodded once before pulling the mule forward and leading him away.

Now what? Where could he go? The revealing ceremony wasn't until the next afternoon and he only hoped nothing happened before then.

Dell turned on his heel and sprinted back into the street. His tired legs took him through the city where shopkeepers were returning home for the night. He kept to the shadows of the buildings, unsure of who might be working with his family.

He passed the road leading to the docks as a carriage he'd recognize anywhere rumbled by, its wheels bouncing on the uneven road.

Why was his family's carriage out in the streets when he doubted his brothers had left the ball?

He ducked out of view to watch it go by, his heart in his throat. He'd never grown to love his brothers, but as a boy, he'd sought their acceptance, never receiving it. Disapproval and disappointment was all he'd known. He hadn't understood.

Until now.

Only one thing mattered to his brothers. It wasn't

family or even wealth as he'd once thought. They cared for no one. But power… they would always want more.

When Dell was brought to them, a bastard mountain boy with no city experience, it had eaten away a bit of their power.

They could let their emotions control them. Dell was proof of their father's weakness.

And he was going to be the downfall of their legacy.

He slipped out of the alcove he'd hidden in and ran until he reached the row of houses belonging to foreign ambassadors.

Edmund's back gate was unlatched, and Dell wondered if there was a purpose to that. How many people came and went from the Belaen man's house in secret? How far into this rebellion was he? He had many spies and loyal men under his control. And Dell now knew why. He understood Edmund on a level he never had before.

Edmund had something—someone—to fight for.

He wrapped his knuckles against the wood of the back door, hoping Edmund's one servant was home and would remember him.

The door opened, and a hand shot out, pulling him inside before slamming the door.

The man who served Edmund with as much loyalty as Dell, pushed him up against the wall. "Why have you come?" The man's wild eyes roamed Dell's face until recognition set in and his grip loosened.

"I want to help," Dell wheezed. "I didn't know where else to go."

The man released Dell and pushed out a breath. "I'm sorry, master Tenyson. I'm a bit on edge tonight."

"We all are. Do you know when Edmund will return?"

He threaded a hand through his hair. "Soon. There are still preparations to be made. You may wait for him."

Dell nodded and walked to the couch before collapsing onto it in exhaustion. He needed to talk to Edmund. To find out what his plan was to protect Helena at the revealing ceremony.

He forced his eyes to stay open as he waited for the one man who could help him keep Helena safe.

Twenty-One

Helena didn't want to be at the ball any longer. Not when she knew something dark was brewing in Madra. Not when Dell left her confused and frightened, thinking something was going to happen to him.

Ian Tenyson slithered to her side once more, and she had to force herself not to shrink away. How could one brother be so sweet and noble while the other was like a slimy serpent?

"Enjoy your stroll, Len?" he asked.

"My name is Helena." She faced him, fire in her eyes. "Princess Helena."

"Your brothers call you Len. If we are to be family, I will have that pleasure as well as many others."

She stepped closer to him, leaning in so their bodies brushed and lowered her voice. "You will never be a part of my family."

She tried to back away, but he gripped her arm. "You think you're clever. But know this *Helena,* your father is not the one who has promised you to me. I will have you."

What did he mean her father didn't promise her in marriage? He was the only person with the power to do so. Not even the queen had a say.

Helena glanced out over the men who'd come for the ball hoping to be chosen. If her father hadn't planned this, maybe one of them did have a chance.

She ripped her arm free of Ian, searching for the one man who could give her answers. Edmund stood with Stev on the edge of the dance floor. No one could tell they were anything more than friends just by looking at them.

But she could see it now that she knew. The small smiles Stev directed Edmund's way told all. Estevan Rhodipus was as serious as they came. But not with Edmund.

"They won't be able to save you," Ian said, brushing the errant strands of hair from her neck.

His touch burned her skin, and she stepped away.

"I don't need them to save me." Her stare could have cut glass. "I can save myself."

She took off across the room, ready to demand Edmund tell her everything. Before she reached him, a line of guards burst into the room, their heavy boots thundering across the marble floor as they formed up. The king followed behind them.

All music ceased. Chatter faded into silence as guests watched the drama unfold.

The king's searing gaze made the crowd step back until he fixed it on his eldest son and the man at his side. "Edmund, Ambassador of Bela, you are under arrest for conspiracy against the crown." He nodded to his guards. "Take him away."

"Father..." Stev glanced from Edmund to the king. "You can't believe Edmund would betray us."

"I need not believe anything, Estevan. I have proof. The guards found explosive powder in his home."

Helena pushed past a guard to arrive at her brother's side. "It's not true." She stepped toward her father and dropped her voice. "Edmund is more loyal than anyone in your guard. If you take him away from us... I promise you'll pay."

She had to make him see. Edmund would protect them against whatever was coming—even against her father. But he couldn't do that from a prison cell.

"Helena," her father barked. "This is the kingdom's business, and a princess has no place in it."

"No place?" She let her voice carry over the enraptured crowd. "I have let you use me my entire life as the symbol of this kingdom. Unattainable. Hidden. Pure. Something that every man should aspire to look upon. Edmund is no traitor." She lifted her hands to the ties at the back of her head. "And I am no symbol."

It happened in slow motion. Priests she hadn't even noticed before ran toward her as her father barked orders.

A few people in the crowd cheered as others gasped.

All Helena heard was the thumping of her own heart as she met Edmund's eyes and removed the mask from her face.

Time stood still as a breeze struck her face, pushing her hair away from her shoulders. Edmund's magic wrapped her in a confident shroud until someone slammed into her, forcing her to the ground and throwing a cloak over her head.

Edmund shouted to the king as two guards dragged him from the room. His words cut off with a muffled grunt. Helena couldn't see what was happening to him.

Two strong arms slid beneath her, keeping the cloak over her face as he lifted her.

The music began again as if nothing had happened.

"She is to be locked in her rooms until we discuss what is to be done," the king commanded.

"Yes, father." Cole. She relaxed, knowing for the moment, she was safe with her brother. He hurried from the room. "Bastard," he muttered. "Bloody bastard."

Helena couldn't refute his words. Her father had proven, once again, he was not on her side. He wasn't even on Madra's side. Only his own.

Edmund. She curled into Cole as a tear slid down her face. She knew what her father did to traitors. He wouldn't be sent to the prison at the monastery. Not yet. Not until he told them everything they wanted to know.

"It's all going to be okay." Cole kicked shut the door to the family wing and removed the cloak from her face.

"How can you say that?" She sniffed. "They have arrested Edmund. I just broke one of the most sacred traditions and father will make me pay for it. Dell…" She shook her head as tears threatened to break free.

"Dell Tenyson?" Cole asked, setting her on her feet. "You've seen him?" He gripped each of her shoulders and bent to look into her eyes. "Where?"

She tried to step back, but he held her in place. "How do you know Dell?" she demanded.

"Ian spoke of him. Was he here? Ian led me to believe he was staying home."

Not liking the accusatory tone in Cole's voice, she twisted out of his grasp. "I need to help Edmund."

"No, you need to let him pay for his crimes."

She couldn't believe what she was hearing. "Cole… It's Edmund. He'd never betray us."

A sneer formed on his lips. "Don't be a fool, Helena. His only loyalty lays with Estevan."

Cole had never spoke to her in such a way and she stumbled away from him. He followed her. "Edmund wants to preserve a reign that should be allowed to crumble. But without him, his people have no leadership, no path forward."

"What are you saying?" Words clogged in her throat as she struggled for breath.

"I needed him out of the way."

She shook her head, tears breaking free. "No."

"He would have ruined everything."

"Cole, you don't know what you're saying."

Remorse shown in his eyes for only a second before it disappeared. His fingers closed around her arm in a bruising grip as he yanked her toward a room at the end of the hall. He pulled a key from around his neck and unlocked the door before shoving her inside.

With one final glance, he shut the door. The grinding of the lock reverberated through the room.

Helena turned, taking in her mother's rooms as the tears she'd been holding back broke free.

"Helena?" a soft voice said, entering from the sitting room.

"Mother." She ran the length of the room before collapsing against the queen, her entire body shaking.

Her mother's arms circled around her. "Helena, it's all going to be okay, I promise you."

"How can you say that? Cole… he…" Her brother's betrayal sliced through her, severing her heart in two. She struggled for breath as sobs stuck in her throat.

Her mother pushed her away and held her at arm's length, dipping her head to look her daughter in the eye. "Listen to me, Lenny girl, they will not defeat us. Your father will make sure of it."

Helena wiped her face and twisted away. "My father?" She stilled her quivering jaw. "The man who allowed the priests to put me in a cell? That father? The man who arrested Edmund when Edmund was the only…" She sucked in a breath and shook her head, realization crashing into her. "He knew."

"Knew what, Helena? Who?"

"Edmund." She'd had her suspicions after what Dell said to her but this went much deeper than she'd thought. "His spies." Had Dell been one of Edmund's spies? Was that why he'd helped her?

"Honey, Edmund was only an ambassador from Bela. Why would he have spies in the city?"

"He was protecting us." She stumbled back until she hit the wooden frame of the bed. Using a hand to guide herself around the post, she sat on the woven quilt. Everything Edmund had done… Everything Dell had done. While the rest of Madra turned against them, Edmund was on their side, risking his life for a crown he cared nothing for, a kingdom that wasn't his own.

Was that what love looked like?

Helena's mother approached her. "Why would Edmund protect us?"

She lifted her gaze. "Because he's the noblest man among us."

Cole. The thought sucked the air from her lungs. She thought she'd been spared the ire he had for Stev and their father. But had he ever loved her at all? Or was he still the orphan boy who arrived at the palace angry at the world?

And now he wanted to take the crown.

Helena shot to her feet. "Stev." The only way to take the crown was to ensure the king and each of his heirs could never again wear it, and to do that…

Understanding lit in the queen's eyes. She'd already come to the same conclusion as Helena. No one was safe. Not anymore.

"Mother, how did they take you from the ball without causing a scene?" she asked.

The queen sighed. "I grew very tired and retreated to my room to await a maid who promised to bring Kassander up. I told my guards they could return to the ball once we were safe in our wing. No one thought the danger would come from within."

From their own family was what she meant, but neither of them said it.

"Where is Kass?" Helena looked to the door in panic. "Why haven't they locked him in here with us?"

"My poor boy." The queen said nothing else in answer as they sat side by side, unable to give each other the comfort they needed.

They didn't know what was happening in the palace

or where her father and Estevan were. Helplessness set in, choking the room in desperation.

"We have to get out of here," Helena whispered.

Her mother reached to take her hand. "Cole won't harm you, Helena. Or Kassander."

She said nothing about herself because they both knew the truth. Cole Rhodipus had no love for the king or queen, and he'd do anything to destroy them.

Twenty-Two

Dell watched Bemus pace the length of the room with the same restlessness he felt. Edmund should have returned hours ago.

"We have to do something." Dell slammed his fist into the table. "To find him."

Bemus' feet froze. "Edmund told me if he were to ever go missing… there's a priest we must find. Koran is loyal to the crown prince and will help us."

Dell shot to his feet. "Then what are we waiting for?"

"Follow me." Bemus led him down a narrow hallway and stopped in front of a worn rug. He lifted the rug, folding it in half to reveal a door in the floor.

Dell's brows drew together. "Edmund has a lot of secrets."

Bemus only nodded as he kneeled to pull the door free. It swung up with a loud creak. Below, a large compartment sunk right into the floor.

"The more I know about Edmund, the more I like

him." Dell gazed over the various weapons hidden in the ambassador's secret stores.

"The king doesn't trust foreigners," Bemus explained. "He orders routine inspections of all the ambassador's homes. Edmund has always been careful. Our most recent inspection was only a day ago, but those men weren't the usual guards. That was one of the ways Edmund knew the rebellion was imminent. He made preparations."

"Preparations?"

"For his arrest. He only hoped it wouldn't be until after your family made their play."

Dell pulled a broadsword free of the weapon's cache, scanning the gleaming steel blade with appreciation.

Bemus put a hand on his arm. "No, sir Tenyson. Walk through the streets with that and people will assume you ride to war."

"Don't we?"

"You don't get it, do you? If we were wrong, and the attack took place tonight, it may very well be over. Our people won't have been in place to stop it. There's a good chance our mission is now one of rescue instead of a battle."

Dell set the sword down heavily, his eyes finding a glass jar of black powder. He recognized it instantly. "What was Edmund doing with this?"

Bemus lifted the jar, preventing Dell from taking it. "A last resort." He found a bag nearby and stuffed it in before handing Dell a long thin sword. "Mercenaries carry these when they aren't marching to battle. No one will look twice at it.

Dell took the sword, balancing it on his hand. "Fine."

He reached for a sword belt and tightened it around his waist before sliding the sword into a scabbard.

Bemus slipped knives into various parts of his clothing before retrieving a long staff.

At Dell's questioning look, he explained. "No one will think me anything but an old man."

Wasn't he just an old man? As quickly as the thought came, it dissipated. Edmund had a purpose in everything he did. Bemus must have been more than he seemed.

They strode from the house to enter the small three-stall stables. One of the horses was missing—most likely at the palace where Edmund had left him.

After saddling both roans, they took off through the streets, never losing sight of the monastery sitting atop a great hill in the distance.

THE GATES of the monastery stood open, but no priests streamed through it. Dell had been to the place only once before when his stepmother sent him to trade for wine. He hadn't enjoyed his visit then, but now an eerie silence settled over the place.

Dell and Bemus inched forward. Dell jerked his head to the large building housing the famed prison. Torches standing along the entry lit it up against the night sky. "Think Edmund is there?"

Bemus nudged his horse toward the prison doors that looked like they'd been blown off their hinges. A black burn stretched up the side of the building.

Dell's eyes flicked to Bemus' saddlebag where the

explosive powder rested, knowing exactly what could cause such destruction.

They slid from their horses to enter the building slowly, acrid air hitting them the moment they stepped inside.

Empty cells stretched down the darkened hall, their metal doors standing open.

"Do you think each floor is the same?" Dell asked.

Bemus only gave him a sideways glance in answer before turning on his heel and leaving the way they'd come.

Outside, Dell sucked in fresh air as if he'd never breathe it again before taking the reins of his horse in hand. He followed Bemus down a worn path toward the center of the monastery compound. A full moon cast the entire place in a silver glow, illuminating their way.

As soon as they rounded the side of the main building, both men froze. The square at the heart of the monastery had been turned into a graveyard. White-robed priests lay sprawled across the cobblestones amid pools of their own blood.

"Dell." Bemus nudged him and pointed toward a column of smoke rising in the distance.

Dell turned back to his horse. "We won't find any help here." He pulled himself up onto his horse as Bemus did the same before the two men thundered back the way they'd come.

As they reached the bottom of the hill, people came running in their direction, their screams jolting through Dell. He dug his heels in and veered around panicked city-dwellers.

Where were Edmund's people? The network he supposedly had throughout Madra.

It wasn't until he reached the palace gates he found his answer.

Half the gate lay in ruins, blown apart by rebels. Amid the fallen stone, royal guards fought rebels. Some of those fighting on the guards' side wore plain clothes. These were the people Edmund had sewn into the very fabric of Madra.

Just like Dell, he'd given them a cause.

Dell jumped from the horse and pulled his sword, wishing Bemus had allowed him to bring the heavier one.

Bemus clamped a hand on his shoulder. "We can't win this, remember that."

"Of course we can," Dell yelled over the screams of people nearby.

"No. Edmund's mission was never about saving Madra or protecting the Rhodipus' reign. He only ever wanted to keep the royal family alive."

The royal family. Dell gazed past the smoking rubble to the steps leading up into the great entryway. He'd never set foot in the palace before the ball, but now it was the only place he could be.

Shouting erupted to his right moments before a blast ripped through the air. The force of it sent Dell flying to his knees. All those who'd been fighting only seconds before now scrambled to get out of the way of a second blast.

The entire world went silent save for the ringing in Dell's ears. He scrambled to his feet, searching for Bemus. Someone ran toward him. A rebel.

Dell braced himself for a fight, but the rebel stopped

in front of him. His wool tunic had been torn halfway down the middle revealing a knife wound he didn't seem to notice. He panted, his lips forming words Dell couldn't hear.

Someone else shook Dell's shoulders, and all sound crashed in on him as if piercing through a veil. A sailor he knew from the docks shouted in his ear. "We have to get into the palace, Dell. Your brothers are already inside with the prince."

The prince?

"Come on, before the fighting starts again." The sailor, one of his stepmother's men, pushed him toward the stairs.

He finally found Bemus, meeting his eyes in silent communication. This was Dell's way in. He tore his gaze away from the only ally he had in this place to sprint up the rubble-strewn steps, past the rebels who were guarding the entrance.

Inside, the hall leading to the ballroom was scattered with overturned tables. A servant in Rhodipus livery lay unmoving in the center, his legs bent unnaturally.

The sailor pushed in front of Dell. "Lord Tenyson's orders were to secure the lower floors one at a time until we can get to the royal family's wing. We have teams on this floor already so we need to join the others upstairs."

He shouldn't have been surprised by the depth of planning his brother had accomplished.

Dell's mind struggled to grasp everything his own family had done.

The walls shook with the force of another explosion outside.

"If they don't stop that soon, they're going to blow up

half the city." The sailor shook his head but Dell would've sworn there was a grin on his face.

Dell glanced back the way they'd come where the people of Madra were dying. Images of the slain priests flashed through his mind.

He'd thought the king was destroying Madra. But then, what was this? It wasn't right.

He picked up his pace, following a cluster of rebels up a wide staircase with golden railings. At the top, a royal guard lay gasping for breath as blood gushed through the spaces in his shining armor. Light from a nearby lantern flickered across his face, his eyes widening in fear as he saw the oncoming rebels.

Dell paused next to him for a moment. He'd been stripped of all weapons. His helmet laid a few feet out of reach.

"What are you doing?" the sailor asked, his lips pulling down into a frown as he looked down on the dying man without sympathy.

"He's going to die." Dell crouched down. "But he need not suffer."

The sailor scrunched his brow as if nothing Dell said made sense. After a tense moment, he shrugged and moved on.

Dell slipped one of Bemus' knives from where he'd hidden it in his shoe and pressed it into the man's hand. He dropped his voice. "You can use this on yourself, or you can take some of these bastards with you when you go. Your choice."

The guard's eyes widened. "Long live the king," he rasped.

Dell squeezed his shoulder. “I wouldn’t go that far, buddy. But the princess is cute, right?”

A weak laugh passed the dying man’s lips. The joke eased some of the tightness in Dell’s chest.

It didn’t work this time.

He met the man’s glassy gaze with a nod before straightening to join the others.

When he searched the hall, it wasn’t the sailor who waited for him.

“Brother,” Reed said. “You shouldn’t be here.”

Twenty-Three

Pain radiated from Helena's shoulder as she slammed it into the door once more. "Cole," she screamed. "Let me out of here!"

"Helena," her mother said calmly. "That will not help."

"He can't keep us in here. We're his family, for priest's sake." She put her hands on her head and turned to her mother. "Family." She walked back to the couch and dropped onto it with a huff. "I feel so useless. I can dance. I can sew. I can sit at royal dinners and not make a fool of myself. If I get close enough, I can take anyone down with a single knife. But when my family needs me most, I can't help them." Her shoulders slumped.

Her mother scooted close and put an arm around her shoulders. "Helena, dear, you are not useless. You have so many skills you have yet to discover. A princess is not all you are. This is not the end for you." She rested her chin on Helena's head. "Besides, I can get us out of here."

Helena reeled back. "What are you talking about?"

Her mother sighed. "In Cana, we were taught so much more than I've passed on to you."

"Of course." The kingdom of spies. She jumped to her feet. "And you didn't think to mention this in the hours we've been sitting in here?"

"I don't want you out there, Len." Sadness etched across her face. "It's killing me to not know where Estevan and Kassander are. You three are my heart. But I do not think it wise any longer to wait and see what they mean to do with us."

She rose to her feet and reached into her hair, pulling free two pins. At the door, she put the pins into the lock, her face a mask of concentration.

It was only when the click of the lock echoed through the room Helena realized she was holding her breath. She exhaled slowly, trying to calm her pounding heart.

The queen walked into her maid's adjoining room, returning with an array of weapons. Helena shouldn't have been surprised at her mother's secrets.

"Helena, you have an advantage. Those at the ball only glimpsed your face. Only your brother and a few select others will recognize you. You must change."

Helena's eyes slid over the blue dress she'd almost forgotten she still wore. Her mother loosened the laces, and the dress fell to the floor, leaving Helena in only her underclothes. She entered the maid's room where a small chest contained a few articles of clothing.

Pulling out a woolen skirt, tight fitting linen shirt, and an apron, she dressed. Her mother worked to unpin her hair before pulling it into the bun favored by servants.

The maid's shoes being three sizes too large and her

mother's too small, she realized she'd have to go barefoot through the halls.

As she walked to the door once more, her hip hit the table, sending its contents to the floor with a crash. The mask she'd left there sailed through the air, the glass pieces shattering on impact.

A small smile lit Helena's face. She was no longer the hidden princess. Maybe after today, she wouldn't be a princess at all. For the first time, she felt like the person she was meant to be.

And that person would fight for her family.

Even if it meant taking down one of her own.

The door burst open moments after the noise, but before Helena could react, her mother flipped a knife in her hand and plunged the tip deep into the rebel's chest. He stumbled back in shock before crumpling to the ground.

The queen pulled her knife free, wiped it clean on her skirt, and extended the hilt toward Helena.

Helena took it tentatively.

"No hesitation, Helena."

She nodded. "No hesitation."

Her mother glanced toward the open door then back to her daughter. "Listen to me, Len. Whatever happens, I love you with my whole heart."

"Mother…" Her words sounded too much like goodbye.

"No, Len. You have to hear this. The throne is not worth protecting. It does nothing but destroy. You… your brothers… you're worth it. Whatever happens, I need you three to make it out of this. Get free of Madra. Make it to Quinn. He'll protect you."

"But Cole…"

Her mother shook her head, fire entering her eyes. "They may be twins, but Quinn is not Cole. Promise me you'll find Kass and Stev and leave this place behind. Promise you won't try to win back the throne. It's not worth your life."

Shouting entered the hall, and Helena fixed her eyes on the open doorway, preparing herself. "I promise."

Without warning, her mother ran into the hall, ball gown whipping around her legs. The sound of steel crashing together was the only thing ringing in Helena's ears as she followed blindly. Her mother twisted and ducked, fighting two rebels at once with a skill Helena had rarely witnessed.

Torches lined the walls and without thinking, Helena pulled one of them free, needing to create a distraction. She held the flame to the edge of the giant tapestry spanning the wall, an image of the royal family—king, queen, four princes and one princess. A happy aura clear on their faces. She set it aflame, knowing those people didn't exist anymore. Maybe they never had.

Flames spread rapidly, and she stood mesmerized by them until her mother pulled her arm. "We must go, Helena."

They passed the bodies of the two men the queen has slain and peered around the corner at the end of the hall. Voices sounded from the sitting room at the center of the royal family's wing. A sitting room the siblings spent countless hours in together.

Helena jerked her head that way, and her mother nodded. They pressed themselves up against the wall and inched forward until they could make out the conversation.

"You were never my father," Cole spat.

"Of course I was." The king coughed.

Helena's wide eyes met her mother's. Father was in there. She scooted forward to peer into the room.

The king kneeled in the center of the room with his hands tied behind his back. Blood trickled from his head.

Cole paced in front of him.

Ian Tenyson sat on the arm of the couch where the Rhodipus children had laughed together and bonded over the years. Where Cole had made promises of protection.

Was everything he'd ever said to her a lie?

"I don't see Kassander or Estevan," her mother whispered, pulling Helena back.

"Or Edmund." Where would they keep the foreign ambassador?

"They won't kill Edmund. Whatever power Cole thinks he has, he'll still fear Bela. Madra would have no chance if they retaliated. No, the ambassador will be sent home."

Helena knew something her mother didn't. Edmund would never leave. Not while Stev was still here.

Ian's voice drifted into the hall. "We need to deal with him, Cole. We gain nothing by drawing it out."

Helena couldn't help but peer into the room again, her breath coming rapidly.

Cole sighed. "Lord Rhodipus, I hereby strip you of the right to rule." He bent and yanked the ring from his father's hand, placing it on his own. "You have betrayed this kingdom."

"You speak of betrayal," the king spat. "What do you think this rebellion of yours is?"

Cole looked him in the eye. "Fewer people will be harmed here today than in one of your wars. Madra can be rebuilt. We can be great again as we once were. On our own. Without foreign influence."

He straightened and held out a hand. A man at the back of the room walked forward and placed a long, thin sword in Cole's open palm.

His finger's curled around it. "I sentence you to death."

The king opened his mouth to speak but his words were cut off as the blade slashed across his throat, spraying crimson life onto the ground as he fell forward.

A scream ripped through Helena. She clapped a hand over her mouth, but it was too late. She'd just witnessed her father's murder and now she was next.

Her mother stood frozen, tears streaming down her face.

"Check the hall," Cole shouted.

A hand clamped on her shoulder jerking her back. Smoke streamed from behind them, evidence of the fire they'd set.

Her mother pulled her into a run, rounding the corner into a room Helena knew well. The tunnels. They could get out. The ornate, unused bedroom sat untouched as if not a part of the palace outside its door.

No. She shook her head. Not without her brothers. Her mother pushed aside the painting hiding the entrance to the tunnels and yanked open the secret door before shoving Helena inside. As the door slammed, cutting off all light, the sounds of a fight broke through the darkness.

Helena sank to her knees, tears tracking down her face. She pounded her fists against the tunnel wall until her knuckles turned bloody.

Her mother was over-matched. She had to be. She counted shouts from four different men, including Cole and Ian.

But it wasn't the noise of battle that killed everything inside her.

It was the silence that followed.

Twenty-Four

Dell's back slammed against the wall as his brother put a hand to his chest. Reed threw a glance over his shoulder to where a group of soldiers ran by.

"Get off me," Dell growled. "Unless you want to arrest me and take me to Ian right now." He held out his wrists. "Come on, brother. Try it."

Reed stared at him for a moment, his eyes narrowing, before someone slammed into him from behind. A soldier in a Madran uniform fought a palace guard.

Reed gripped the collar of Dell's shirt and yanked him out of the way, pulling him through an open doorway and kicking it shut behind them.

He released Dell with a shove. "What are you doing here, Dell? Edmund promised me you'd be on the ship leaving Madra."

Confusion warred with rage inside Dell as he stared at the brother who'd never had a kind word for him. Reed followed Ian's lead in everything he did. The two of them had tormented him since the day he arrived in the city.

Dell wiped sweat and ash from his face. "Why do you care? You got what you've always wanted. You and Ian. Is your mother involved in this too? Being the tip of the spiral wasn't enough for you. You wanted more. More influence. More power."

Reed slumped against the wall. "Sometimes there is no other choice. And no, mother didn't want to be involved. She didn't come to the ball tonight."

Dell advanced on him. "Of course there's another choice." He looked to the door. "Why are Madran soldiers fighting royal guards?"

"The army has chosen their side."

Dell deflated. Then Madra really was lost. His brother had won. With the army behind the rebels, Edmund had never had any chance to stop this fight.

"Where is Edmund?" he asked, meeting his brother's pained gaze.

Reed pushed himself away from the wall. His stocky frame ambled across the room as he paced in front of the long table near the wall. Buckets of cutlery and stacks of plates lined the surface. Dell took in the room as he waited. It must have been where servants prepared to serve the royal family. A large cherry wardrobe sat partially open at the far end, the corner of an apron hanging out.

Normal. The room spoke of normalcy in the palace. Life went on, and soon these servants would serve a new king.

"Reed." He grit his teeth. "No more stalling. Tell me where Edmund is. And the royal family."

Reed's feet froze, but he didn't turn to face Dell. "Edmund was arrested at the ball. He's being kept under guard in one of the rooms in the king's wing."

Dell's mind tried to process Edmund's captivity. He'd be no help to them now. But Len… "And the royal family?" He swallowed past the thickness in his throat.

Reed finally turned, darkness swirling in his gaze. "Ian has… plans for them."

A whimper came from the direction of the wardrobe, and both men paused, listening for any other sound. Footsteps stomped through the hall outside the door amid shouting voices, but the soft cry was all they focused on.

Reed approached the wardrobe cautiously and pushed the door open wider. He reached in between the hanging aprons and uniforms. A high pitch yelp sounded as he pulled a young boy free.

Dark curls fell over wide eyes as the boy tried to pull away from Reed.

Recognition sparked in Dell. "Your Highness."

Fire entered the boy's gaze, and he lifted his quivering chin, trying to be tough even as he stood before them in a child's sleeping gown. "Unhand me."

"You heard the kid." Dell put a hand on his brother's shoulder. "Let him go."

Reed loosened his grip.

"I am Kassander Rhodipus," the young prince stated. "Are you going to kill me?"

"We don't kill children." Reed pressed his fingers against his closed eyes.

"Does Ian know that?" Dell asked, his eyes scanning the kid who looked so very much like Helena. "What do you think is going to happen when he gets his hands on the entire royal family? The only way to cement the bastard prince's rule is to make sure all his siblings are in the ground."

The bravado in Kassander's stance cracked and his eyes glassed over. "Cole won't hurt me."

"I wish I had as much faith as you, little prince." Dell walked to the wardrobe to rummage through it until he found what he wanted. He draped a dark cloak over Kassander's shoulders. There was no way he could just leave him. Not when he gazed up at him with Len's hazel eyes. "I'm taking the prince. If you want to arrest him, you'll have to take us both."

Dell spared one more long look for his brother, waiting for him to make a move. Instead, Reed turned and opened the door, disappearing into the shadows once more.

Dust rained down as another explosion struck.

"People are pouring through the gates," a soldier yelled as he ran by. "All those loyal to the king are called to fight."

Kassander tried to take off, but Dell held him back.

"They need us to fight," Kassander yelled.

Dell watched more soldiers rush by. Not palace guards, but military men and women. "I don't think the king they mention is your father."

"I remember you," Kassander said. "From the docks… and the games. You're a Tenyson. I'm not going anywhere with you, Rebel."

Dell didn't have time for this. He turned on his heel, gripping the boy's shoulders and bent to look him in the eye. "You don't have another option, kid. I'm not going to kill you, but I have one goal… to get Helena out of here alive. Come or don't, that's your choice."

He released the prince and joined the chaos snaking through the halls. Blood stained the velvet carpeting. Furniture lay in broken pieces. Wall hangings were slashed and torn.

The palace was a war-zone.

"Dell." Kassander pointed to a group of men and women in armor marching down the hall.

Dell pulled Kassander back into the shadows of a doorway as they watched the man who'd betrayed his own family for the crown pass by, blood spattered across his face.

Kassander's entire body shook and Dell realized for the first time, he wasn't so different from the royal family after all. Warring siblings. Betrayal. It didn't matter if you lived in a palace or a loft in the stables, it all hurt the same.

Ian strode beside Cole, and they stopped as they came upon another guard. After they spoke a few words, they marched toward the stairs that would take them to the main level where the explosions were growing.

Dell pulled Kassander forward. "We need to get to the royal residence and find Edmund. He'll help us."

Kassander veered to the right into a hall flooded with light. Smoke seeped out under a door at the end.

"No guards," Dell whispered to himself. "Cover your face, kid."

Dell pressed his arm against his mouth and pushed the door open. Smoke curled around the ornate sitting room, choking the air from it.

Did they leave Edmund to die among flames?

Dell ran forward, stopping when he caught sight of

the fire blazing along the tapestries on the wall. "Kassander, stay back," he yelled.

His eyes stung as he forced open the first door he saw. Empty.

Kassander's scream echoed through his mind, and he ran back the way he'd come to find a Madran soldier with a knife to Kassander's throat. Dell pulled his knife free as he met the boy's eyes, but before he could make a move, an arrow split through the attacker's head, right between the eyes.

The knife he held nicked Kassander's neck, drawing a bead of blood, before the man fell back away from the prince.

Dell prepared to fight whoever appeared to take the prince. A figure emerged in the smoke with two others behind him.

"Stev!" Kassander cried, flinging himself at his brother.

Prince Estevan didn't take his eyes from Dell. "Are you going to put that down?" He gestured to the knife Dell continued to aim at him. "Dell Tenyson, Edmund trusts you, but I'd feel more comfortable if you didn't try to stab me or the few guards who've chosen the right side in this." He gestured to the men behind him.

Dell lowered the knife. Coughs racked his body, and he covered his mouth to keep the smoke at bay. "Where is Edmund? Have you seen him?"

Estevan shook his head. "One of my men said he's here along with the rest of my family." He moved closer.

Black grit streaked down the prince's face and exhaustion lined his eyes. He breathed out, coughing as he inhaled more smoke. "We need to find them before it's too late."

Neither of them said what they were thinking as smoke swirled around them and the light of the flames flickered across the room.

It might already be too late.

Twenty-Five

The quiet of the tunnel sucked all life from Helena. She didn't know what was going on in the palace or if her family was okay.

No one was coming to save her.

That thought swirled round and round in her mind until it latched on, refusing to break free.

No one was coming to save her.

So, she'd have to save herself.

She felt for the knife her mother had given her, its solid weight a comfort against the ice in her veins.

They killed her father. Probably murdered her mother. They would have no one else she loved.

Helena pushed to her feet. She had to get back to the royal residence to confront her brother.

She brushed her hands down the maid's skirt she wore. No one would know her for anything other than a servant. Except Cole. He'd see her coming for him.

She'd always thought she had an unbreakable bond

with her brothers. They were the ones who would always be on her side.

But now she knew the truth. That bond had been made of glass—easy to shatter and impossible to repair.

Just like their kingdom.

Because after tonight, Madra would never be the same.

She listened with her ear pressed to the door for a moment, hearing nothing on the other side. As she pushed into the familiar room, her mother's face greeted her, lifeless and pale.

A sob stuck in her throat. Chloe Rhodipus was more than her father ever deserved, and it wasn't until her death Helena felt she finally knew her mother.

She'd saved her.

Helena bent to touch her mother's forehead, avoiding the pool of blood surrounding her. "I won't let you down, Mother. I'll find Kassander and Stev if it's the last thing I do."

She straightened and strode into the hall with purpose, her knife clutched tightly in one hand.

A rebel soldier passed nearby, and she pressed herself to the wall. As soon as he was right in front of her, she lunged, tackling him to the ground.

His strong hands gripped her, trying to push her off, but she locked her legs around his chest and pressed the tip of her knife up under his ribs. He weakened gradually as she slid it in until he stilled altogether.

She scrambled off him, pulling her dripping knife free.

"One less traitor," she said to herself.

But her chest didn't feel any less tight. There was no

relief in taking the rebel's life. She flicked her eyes to her bloodied hands, which she no longer recognized.

She had to move.

As she rounded the corner, she stopped. Two guards stood outside the door to a meeting room her father had rarely used.

Why were they guarding it?

There was something in there they didn't want taken. Or someone.

No one will recognize you.

Her mother's words helped her form a plan. Sending up a thank you to the mask she'd always hated, she slipped the knife up her sleeve and ran.

"Help me," she cried when she reached the rebel guards. She gripped the closest one's arm. "I was only doing what the new king asked—searching for the young prince—when a group of men in royal armor started chasing me." Her eyes widened, and she sucked in a breath as if she'd just run through the entire palace.

The two guards looked to one another and then down the hall where no pursuers appeared.

"Please," she pleaded, her fingers still gripping one of their arms.

New plan. This wasn't working. Helena's mind spun as she blinked rapidly. Whoever was being guarded in that room was most likely an ally.

Two rebels appeared around the corner, stopping when they saw her with the rebel guards.

"What do we have here, Astor?" one of them asked.

Astor must have been the guard whose arm she still held because the new arrival flicked his eyes to her hand before settling on her face. He smirked.

She removed her hand, using it to push her sticky hair from her sweat-dampened forehead. Her heart thundered in her ears as they neared.

Four rebels now surrounded her, and she finally understood why her father never let her out of the palace. Madra was a dangerous place. People always wanted to take things from those who had them.

In order to face the perils, one had to become dangerous themselves.

Helena rose up to her whole height—which, granted, was still much shorter than their muscular builds. But the look she gave them could have cut glass.

"I have orders." She slipped the knife from her sleeve into her palm. "You will allow me to see the prisoner."

If the guards were surprised at her sudden change in demeanor, they didn't show it. Astor grinned. "Yeah, well we have orders too." They closed in around her, cutting off any escape.

Helena sucked in a shaky breath, refusing to let the fear coursing through her show on her face. She clenched the knife so tightly it bit into her skin.

But the pain only reminded her why she was here.

They'd killed her father. Murdered her mother. For all she knew, Stev and Kass had joined them in the after.

A Madran princess experienced a transformation on the night of her name day ball. It was meant to change her from child to woman in the hearts and eyes of the people.

It was the day they were truly revealed to the world.

Hours ago, she'd ripped off her mask, but the transformation was now. No longer a princess of a kingdom she already knew her family had lost. Never to be royal again.

All she had left was the burning revenge inside her heart.

She flipped the knife into her other hand, light from the torches dancing across the ornate steel blade.

One of the rebels laughed. "I don't think this one is on our side, boys." He leaned in. "I was there, you know. When they took the young prince." He drew a line across his throat with his thumb.

"You're lying," she lunged.

He jumped back. "Why are you loyal to a royal family who cares nothing for you?"

She swiped with the knife, and he gripped her wrist to stop its arc.

"When they brought Estevan Rhodipus to his knees," he whispered. "I saw fear in the great warrior."

"You lie." Hot tears burned her eyes.

"Callum." One of the other rebels said in warning. "Let's just put her out of the palace."

"No." Callum's grip tightened on Helena's wrist until she feared it would break. "She should hear what happens to those who betray Madra. Then you can go into the city and tell others what their disobedience gets them."

She ground her teeth against the pain. "You're the traitors."

Callum shook his head. "Oh, you should have seen it. The princess… we always knew she must have a pretty face beneath that mask, but she looked like an angel as her own brother took her life."

The words ricocheted through her mind. The

princess? Every word they said was a lie. They had to be. Maybe Stev and Kass were okay after all.

White-hot rage rose from the darkest pits of her soul, burning out every bit of mercy she had inside her. She twisted her wrist so suddenly he released her.

Without hesitation, she lunged for him, burying her knife in the soft flesh above his collarbone. Blood gurgled from his lips as strong hands pulled her away and shouts erupted.

Callum stumbled back before falling against the wall and sliding to the ground. He didn't move again.

Astor wrapped an arm around Helena's neck while the other guard drew his sword. The rebel who'd arrived with Callum bent to check his pulse.

"She killed him," he said, surprise tingeing his voice.

Helena strained against Astor's hold, jerking her head back to crack it against his chin. His arms only tightened as a curse left his mouth.

The second guard closed in as he brought his sword up to press the tip to Helena's chest. All breath left her as the seconds ticked by.

She lifted her eyes to meet her captors' in defiance. If this was how it ended, she would not make it easy. The other plain-clothed rebel watched with eagerness flashing across his face.

Was this a game to them?

Did the rebels take joy in destroying everything her family had built?

She kicked her heel back, connecting with Astor's leg above his kneecap.

"Dammit," he growled, his warm breath blowing across her neck.

The next words that left his mouth were so quiet, she almost thought she imagined them.

"Trust me."

Trust him? Trust *him*?

He had to be kidding.

"We're not killing the girl," Astor said.

The rebel stood and backed away from his dead friend on the ground. "She killed Callum," he growled. "Are you telling me her life is worth more than his?"

Astor paused, frozen for only a moment in time, before he shoved her to the side, knocked away the other guard's blade and pulled his own. "I'm saying it's worth more than yours."

"Traitor," the man yelled before the tip of a sword protruded from his belly.

Astor twisted to avoid being split in two as the second guard raised a giant broadsword. With an agility that only small men had, he lunged toward the rebel who was still gasping for breath and pulled his weapon free before rounding on his fellow guard.

Their blades clashed, sending the ring of steel echoing down the hall.

Helena backed away until her back hit the door. She inched sideways to where her knife protruded from Callum's neck and yanked it free. Blood sprayed from the wound, splattering across her face. She wiped it, her sleeve coming away stained with crimson.

She clutched the knife to her chest. That was two. She'd killed two people now.

But she knew there would be more. It was for her family. There was no other choice.

The guard's fight ended with Astor slicing his blade

through a gap in the underarm of the other guard's armor. He collapsed to the ground and was still sputtering for life when Astor bent to rip a ring of keys from his belt.

Helena tried to back away, almost forgetting about whoever was in that room, as Astor's eyes found hers.

"Don't move," he growled with a shake of his head. "I've been standing here for the past hour waiting for a distraction that would stall the rebels who were sent to check on us every quarter hour. But you… we have little time because others will have heard the fight."

She didn't know what was going on, but as he jammed the key into the lock, she couldn't move.

He opened the door, and she gasped, covering her mouth with her hand.

"Edmund."

She tried to run forward, but Astor blocked her way.

Edmund sat slumped in a metal chair in the corner of the darkened room. Shackles ringed his ankles, chaining him to two iron hooks on the wall. Blood-streaked blonde hair stuck to the bruises on his face.

Hours.

She'd seen him only hours ago.

"My brother will pay for this," she said to herself.

Astor grunted. "The rebels found him in this state." He glanced at her out of the corner of his eye. "This was your father's work."

Her face dampened with tears of betrayal. Neither side in this fight was worth dying for. It was the only thing she knew.

Just as her mother said, her family was more important than any crown.

And Edmund was as much family as anyone.

She pushed past Astor to stop at Edmund's side. He lifted his head as if noticing her for the first time. "Len." A smile slid across his face. "How good of you to come."

"What's wrong with him?" She looked to Astor for answers.

The lithe guard shut the door, entombing them in the dimly lit, bare room. "They've drugged him. We were set to give him a new dose soon so it should be wearing off. It was the only way to keep him compliant."

"How is he still alive?" She cupped his face gently, examining each bruise.

"Killing him would put us at odds with Bela."

Understanding lit in her. "And the only thing Cole truly fears is magic." Her foot hit the chains snaking across the ground and bile rose in her throat. "Get them off him. Now!"

Edmund looked as if he didn't understand why she yelled, but her entire body trembled.

Astor flipped through the keys before bending to unlock the shackles.

Edmund stood as soon as he was free and Helena pulled him to her, burying her face in his chest. His arms came around her. "Lenny, what's wrong?"

"Everything," she sobbed.

He rested his chin on her head. "Let's find the queen. She can make you some tea."

Helena's chest constricted.

Edmund looked to the guard who had yet to say a word to him. "Astor." He grinned. "Nice of you to visit, but I don't remember calling you from your mission among the rebel troops. Was it Estevan?"

"Sir," Astor began. "The rebels have taken the palace."

"Not possible." Edmund released Helena and scratched his jaw. He furrowed his brow, clarity returning to his eyes. "Our sources had the date set for tomorrow."

"They were wrong."

"Come on, Edmund." Helena placed a hand on each of his arms and peered up into his face. "Come back to us. Clear away the fog. Find your magic again. We need you." She paused. "Stev needs you."

His eyes snapped to hers. "Stev…"

"We don't know where he is. The king and queen…" She swallowed thickly, forcing herself to say the words. "Are gone. But I refuse to leave this palace before we find Stev and Kass."

"Stev." He said the name almost like a prayer, and his shoulders went rigid. He blew out a breath and closed his eyes.

A gust of air whipped Helena's bangs from her face. She smiled for the first time since the ball. Edmund was back.

The wind settled before disappearing altogether as if Edmund's magic wasn't there at all.

Edmund strode to the door and yanked it open only to stop as four swords blocked his way. Ian Tenyson stepped forward.

"Hello, princess." He smirked. "I said I would have you and I never break my promises." He turned to his guards. "The girl comes with us. Arrest the ambassador. Kill the traitor."

Twenty-Six

Dell fell through the door into the servants' stairwell from the royal family's residence, smoke chasing him from the row of once grand rooms.

Nothing. They'd found nothing. No one alive at least. Anyone who'd been trapped in the wing was either dead or found some way to escape.

They'd found the king with his throat cut lying in a pool of his own blood. His cruel eyes no longer saw the destruction he'd created.

Because Dell had no doubt in his mind, this rebellion was the king's fault.

The young prince Kassander landed next to Dell with a thump as his brother threw him from the flames they left behind.

Coughs wracked Dell's body as he bent over, gasping for breath.

"We need to get lower," Estevan wheezed. "Away from the smoke."

Dell clambered to his feet. *Helena, where would you have gone?*

He didn't have time to think of anything but escaping the heat and poisonous air they left behind. His feet thundered down the steps and he gripped a carved golden rail to keep from falling face first into the darkness.

The air grew clearer the farther from the smoke they ran, and Dell sucked it in as if he'd never tasted anything so sweet.

Kassander stumbled, his weak legs giving out beneath him. He collided with Dell, sending him tumbling down the last few steps and landing at the bottom in a heap.

Every muscle in Dell's body screamed in agony as he tried to roll the boy off him. *Keep going. You have to keep going.*

Sounds of fighting reached them and Dell met Estevan's gaze. "Takes two sides to fight."

Estevan nodded. "We probably have allies out there."

Estevan bent and lifted his brother. Did that man ever tire? Did the smoke in his lungs have no effect?

Dell rolled with a groan. Why'd he return to the palace on this night? He could have been safely away on a ship headed for Bela.

Oh, right… there was a girl.

As if the thought of her brought forth his strength, he pushed himself from the floor and pulled the thin sword from its scabbard. Wiping soot from his face, he turned to the prince.

"You're going to need your hands to fight, prince." He gestured to the unconscious boy in Estevan's arms.

Estevan leaned his face down to listen to the boy's chest. "He's breathing." He glanced around at the small room at the bottom of the stairs. The only light came through the cracked open door.

He set his brother down in the far corner, pain twisting on his face as he stared at the boy. "I'm coming back for you, Kass," he whispered. "I promise." He dropped a kiss onto the boy's ashy hair and straightened to regard Dell. "I hope you know how to handle that thing more than the carving knife you threatened me with, boy."

Dell bristled at the term 'boy' but now was not the time to argue with an arrogant prince. This time, they were on the same side.

Coughing the last bit of smoke from his lungs, Dell shouldered the door aside and charged into the back hall, normally used only by those serving the royal family.

He leaped at the still form of a young girl in Rhodipus livery, her light hair circling her head like a ring of light.

Rebels fought those servants who took up their king's name. Royal soldiers fought royal guards.

Stev jumped into the melee without a second thought, swinging his long sword at those he could hack his way through.

"It's the prince," someone yelled. Dell didn't know which side recognized the prince first, but it was a galvanizing call. Rebels wanted the reward they'd receive for capturing the true heir and delivering him to the pretender. Loyalists cleaved to the Rhodipus line as if Madra would fall apart without them.

Maybe it would.

Or maybe their demise would finally allow Madra to flourish.

Dell didn't care. The rebels stood in the way of him finding the princess. Bemus appeared among the fray with the first signs of true life Dell had seen from the man who'd lost so much. He parried and kicked one leg out, using his foot to hook his opponent's knee and take him down before ramming his sword into the rebel's belly.

Cries of pain mixed with grunts of effort. Dell advanced to Bemus' side, blocking an oncoming blow. The force reverberated up his arm as he was locked in a duel of strength with a narrow-eyed opponent.

He pushed the man's sword away, and it clattered to the ground. Dell lost his grip on his own blade, but didn't waste a moment as he dove at the rebel, knocking him to the ground.

His fists beat into his opponent's face with every bit of viciousness he possessed. This was who he was. Not a dueler with fancy swords or formal training. A brawler. A boxer who preferred street fights to the ring.

By the time the man stilled, Dell's knuckles ran red. As he jumped to his feet to help Stev, a scream ripped through the air, tearing the world in two.

Helena.

Len.

His eyes flicked to Estevan who battled two men. Bemus held his own alongside a squad of royal guards.

"Dell," Estevan yelled as he twisted to avoid another blow.

Dell met his burning stare. What did he see there? Permission? A plea? An order?

"That's my sister, Dell." Desperation. Something he'd never expect from the prince. "Get her out of the palace. Please."

An attacker advanced on Dell, but he ducked away, sprinting toward the entry to the main hall. Smoke no longer clouded his mind or choked his breath. Every pain he'd felt faded away. A new energy chased the exhaustion away.

"I'm coming, Len," he said, mostly to himself.

He entered the hall cautiously, preparing himself for anything he saw.

Three men stood over a kneeling man and woman. Recognition burned into him as he realized Len and Edmund had their arms tied behind their backs.

Tears made tiny tracks through the blood on Len's face, but no fear shone in her eyes.

"You're going to pay for this, Ian," she growled.

Dell snapped his eyes to the men he hadn't truly looked at yet. His brother stood in the center of two broad-shouldered rebels. Two dead men and two dead women lay sprawled across the ground.

Dell advanced silently, letting the shadows hide his approach.

Ian laughed as he bent forward, his face only inches from Len's. "I may not be allowed to kill you, Helena, but Cole didn't say anything about harming this pretty face." His fingers trailed down her cheek. "It's a shame you had to hide it for so long." His hand inched down her neck and over the bodice of her dress.

She sat impossibly still.

Edmund fought against his restraints. "Don't touch her."

Ian straightened. "Shame you care more for her than your precious Camille of Gaule."

A growl ripped from Edmund's throat. "What have you done with Camille?"

A smirk splashed across the asshole's face. "Nothing, of course. She is to fulfill the promise of her kingdom. Madra will have a Gaulean princess as queen and the Gaule army as allies. The treaty drawn up makes no mention of which Madran heir she must marry."

Ian patted the side of Edmund's face. "Cole will be a better husband to her than Estevan, isn't that right, Edmund?"

Edmund snapped his teeth, and Ian yanked his hand away with a muttered "rabid dog."

Dell slid a knife free of his belt, trying to decide how to make his move. He'd be no match against Ian and his men. Estevan and Bemus were still fighting back in the servants' hall.

Ian gripped Edmund's hair, forcing his head to the side to expose his neck. He held out his hand and one of his men set a knife upon his palm. Ian took it and pressed the tip to Edmund's skin just below his ear.

The ambassador didn't even flinch.

"Neither side trusts you, Edmund of Bela. The king you defend had you beaten in his paranoid quest to find those who would do him harm."

"I defend no king," Edmund spat.

Ian pressed the knife harder, drawing a line of blood. "Interesting." He removed the knife and wiped the blood with his thumb before drawing a crimson line down Edmund's forehead. "You fight for no king… yet still you act against us, Madra's rescuers."

"You rescue no one," Helena growled.

Ian issued a quick kick to her side. "I'm not speaking

to you. You'll learn to obey me once we're wed." A threat deepened his voice.

"You think you're on the right side in this, Ian Tenyson." Edmund lifted his eyes. "But I have been through war. I have seen kingdoms torn apart from within and enemies on the outside. War doesn't heal. It only destroys. There is only one side here. Madra's. And if you insist on rebellion, you act against the freedom you say you're fighting for."

Ian's knee collided with Edmund's chest and the blonde man fell sideways with a grunt of pain. "The Rhodipus line and their precious priests caused this, Edmund. Not us."

Edmund lay on his side, unable to rock himself back to his knees. As his eyes scanned the hall, and they connected with Dell's from his place hidden in the shadows.

He flicked his gaze from Helena to Dell. What was he trying to tell him?

Dell stepped forward, sword in one hand, knife in the other, but before he could make a move, the sound of many heavy boots entered the hall, stealing all chance of saving Helena and Edmund.

Ian's new ally strode up beside him, a frown marring his face.

Cole Rhodipus had arrived.

TWINE CUT into Helena's wrists as she stared up at the brother she'd revered only yesterday. Every one of her brothers had been heroes to her. No flaws. No weaknesses. They protected her and provided a barrier between her and their father.

She'd never thought she'd need protection from one of them.

Her mother's face flashed before her eyes, and all love she had for Cole drifted away on a current of hatred and desperation.

Ian Tenyson stood at his side. Her father's old ally fixed an intense gaze on her, cocking his head to the side as if he couldn't quite figure something out. He looked to Edmund who lay beside her and seemed to stare off into the shadows.

"Sister," Cole began.

Her lip curled. "Don't call me that. I am not your sister. Not anymore."

She'd have sworn she saw sadness pass his features, but he shook it away. "Whatever you may think of me, Len, I do love you."

"Just not mother and father, right?" Hot tears burned her eyes.

Cole sighed. "She was not my mother." He put a hand on Helena's shoulder. "But I know you loved her. I am sorry for that."

"Don't touch me." She jerked away, wishing more than anything to have a knife within reach.

He retracted his fingers and curled them into a fist. Ian whispered something in his ear before he marched toward an arch that obscured part of the hall from view.

A struggle sounded and Cole nodded to two of his guards to go assist Ian. They took off, pulling a young man from the shadows and disarming him.

"Dell," Helena whispered.

Edmund rolled into a sitting position, his eyes scanning Dell. Helena couldn't let them take him too. Without thinking, she jumped to her feet, her tied wrists making it difficult, and ran at the guards holding Dell. They weren't able to reach for their weapons before she slammed her shoulder into the one on the right. Both released Dell.

"Go!" she screamed at Dell.

He scrambled to his feet and tried to urge her along after him, but pain ripped into her shoulder, searing down her arm as if her entire body cracked open.

"Stop," Cole yelled, but his voice was only a wisp of sound in the haze of her mind. Her knees buckled and Dell caught her before they slammed into the marble floor.

"Someone help," Dell called.

"Len!" Edmund tried to get to her, but his way was blocked and he couldn't reach for a weapon with his hands tied.

Cole crouched over her, his eyes the stormy gray she'd always loved. They spoke of passion. Of fight.

She blinked away tears as numbness spread through her body like a tidal wave, taking everything in its path.

Cole pointed to the man who'd thrown the knife. "Arrest him. He harmed the princess against my orders to leave her intact."

In the last moments before the darkness swallowed her whole, she almost thanked him for looking out for her.

Twenty-Seven

Dell held Len's lifeless body in his arms, her blood soaking into the sleeves of his shirt.

"Len," he said, tears choking his voice. "Len." He pressed his forehead to hers. "Please don't leave me."

"Fetch me a healer," Cole ordered. "Now. If my sister dies, I will have each one of your heads."

Two of his soldiers ran off to find a healer, but Dell barely noticed them leave.

Cole pierced him with a dark gaze. "You're the Tenyson bastard."

"He's no Tenyson," Ian spat.

"That's what my father said about me for the first ten years of my life." Cole stayed quiet for a moment, brushing his hand over Len's head. "Are you loyal to your family?"

"He's never—" Ian stopped abruptly when Cole raised his hand.

If Dell said no, he had no doubt Cole would cut him

down right where he sat. But if he said yes… would that betray everything he was?

Instead of answering, he lowered his eyes to Helena's serene face. "She's going to be okay." He wasn't speaking to anyone but himself, yet Cole put a hand on his shoulder. For just a moment, they were in their grief together.

Ian shifted where he stood. "If she dies, you owe me a wife."

A roar ripped from Cole's throat and he turned to Ian. "I owe you nothing."

Dell tried to take pleasure in his brother's chastisement but he couldn't focus on anything but the girl in his arms.

Cole cut strips of his own shirt with a knife and handed them to Dell. Dell pulled the knife free from the right side of her chest and pressed the cloth to it. He dropped the knife, and it clattered to the ground.

Dell pressed two fingers to her neck to feel her heart thumping against them.

Edmund bucked against the rebel holding him back, freeing himself to run to Helena's side.

A door crashed open, spilling loyalists into the hall. They froze when they saw the scene now playing out.

Dell lifted his eyes to find Estevan and Bemus leading their followers forward.

Around him, guards braced for a fight. But not Dell. He held Len tighter against his chest. Edmund took her hand as his glassy eyes found Estevan.

"Are you going to make me fight you, brother?" Estevan asked. He scanned the group, his eyes landing on Helena and widening before returning to Cole. "Why her,

Cole? Why Len? I know how you've always felt about mother, father, even me… but Helena? She loved you more than any of us and you…" His voice grew thick. "She was good. And now she's—"

"Not dead," Dell said, his words echoing down the hall. "Not dead."

Estevan's shoulders dropped. "Not dead?"

Edmund met the prince's eyes and shook his head.

They stayed locked in a silent communication. Edmund mouthed the word "no".

Estevan nodded. "I'm sorry, Edmund." He faced his brother. "I want this to end."

Cole crossed his arms over his chest. "I'm listening."

"The palace you fought so hard for is crumbling. People continue to battle through the night. The fire engulfing the royal residence will spread if not contained."

"All things we are aware of, Stev. Tell me why I should negotiate with you instead of run you through with my sword."

"I'll surrender."

"Stev," Edmund groaned. "You can't do this."

Estevan ignored his protest. "I will allow you to take my throne and my person. You can do as you wish with me. Make an example. Kill me. I won't fight it. I'll tell the loyalists to stand down and begin repairing their kingdom. No more fighting. No more destruction."

Cole narrowed his eyes. "What do you want in return?"

Estevan stepped forward, fire burning in his gaze. "Release them. All of them. Edmund. Helena.

Kassander. Dell. Allow them to leave Madra. It's the only way to complete your takeover of the throne. The people will never move past the unrest as long as they fight for me."

"You can't possibly be considering this," Ian snapped at Cole. "You promised Helena to me."

"Shut up." Cole commanded.

The rebels returned with a graying healer in tow. Dell clutched Helena tighter, refusing to let her go. Dell scanned the healer's gaunt face. Deep lines were carved into his skin. He moved past Cole and Stev in their now silent standoff and dropped to his knees slowly.

"I am healer Whiston," he stated. "Let me see the princess."

Dell finally relinquished his hold on her to turn her small frame, revealing the deep wound in her shoulder. Red seeped free of the gash, spreading out through the fabric of her bodice.

Healer Whiston leaned in, peering at it for only a moment before lifting his eyes to the new king. "Fatal, I'm afraid."

No emotion coated his words, but they had the impact of a thousand battering rams driving the destruction from the inside out. Dell shook his head, unable to believe it. Not wanting to see this as the end.

Cole cleared his throat, fighting back his own feelings. "I accept your terms, Estevan Rhodipus. With Helena passing into the after, the rest of them mean nothing to me." He turned away from his remaining family. "I will allow you to say goodbye. Dell will be allowed to leave with Helena and Kassander. I cannot let Camille join them, however. We will use Edmund's gift to get your message out to the people and then he will be free to leave as well."

"No," Edmund's voice cut through the tension like glass. "I can't. I'm not leaving you." His eyes pleaded with Estevan as Cole began walking away.

Estevan dropped to his knees in front of Edmund. "I once asked you to keep my family safe from rebellion. We didn't know the threat would come from inside. But I need to ask this of you again. Protect Kass as if he was your own blood. I wouldn't trust anyone else with his life."

Tears streamed down Edmund's face and he pressed his forehead against Estevan's. "What is he going to do to you, Stev?" He closed his eyes. "I have this feeling I'm never going to see you again and that…" He sucked in a breath. "I love you."

Estevan brushed Edmund's tears away with his thumbs and pressed his lips to the Belaen's. "You brought me to life, Edmund of Bela. I may be headed toward my own execution, but I will be grateful to you until the day I die."

Dell wiped his own tears away. So, this was how it ended. A dead king and queen. A murdered princess, and a captured prince.

Estevan pulled back. "Find Quinn. He'll help you keep them safe."

Them. *Them.* Dell stared into Helena's pale face. She didn't need to be kept safe any longer.

Guards hauled Estevan to his feet and formed up around him.

As another gripped Edmund's arm and yanked him forward, he met Dell's watery gaze. "Get Helena and Kassander to the docks. Bemus will help you. If they had word of the rebellion, the ship would have waited for us."

The ship. *Corban.*

This wasn't the end after all. If he made it in time.

Twenty-Eight

The final look Cole Rhodipus gave his sister would be forever burned into Dell's mind. Eyes blazing with both fury and desperation as he watched her breathing slow. A jaw clenching and unclenching as he fought to keep any emotion from flickering across his face.

It was painfully obvious to anyone who watched him.

He may have hated his lot in life, but his sister had existed outside of the burning embers of his pain. She'd been the light in the otherwise dark world.

Dell knew because she acted as the same guiding force for him. And they were both going to lose her.

Cole issued orders to his men to escort Dell from the palace along with the near-dead princess. Estevan bent to kiss her cheek, a single tear breaking the facade of strength he emitted.

"Go." Edmund's voice thickened. "I'll be there soon. Make sure she stays with us, Dell. Don't you lose her."

He only nodded, the words he wanted to say clogging in his throat.

He'd come to the palace to protect Helena. No other reason. And he'd failed. But he wouldn't fail in this.

Bemus disappeared with one of the guards, returning a moment later with the half-conscious Kassander cradled in his arms.

A second guard attempted to lift Len from Dell's lap.

"No." Dell shifted Len to the ground and stood. He couldn't stand the thought of rebel hands on her. He bent, sliding one arm underneath her back and the other under the bend in her legs. Her hair fell loose of her bun and fell in wild waves over his arm.

"Keep pressure on her wound," Bemus said, leaning in. "And don't let any of them know she still lives."

Dell nodded, wedging the ball of cloth against him to keep it pressed to the gash as Helena's life continued to seep from her.

Cole's rebel soldiers surrounded them, marching through the halls. The fighting outside had mostly died down, but tiers of smoke rose from sections of the wall surrounding the courtyard. A giant hole now stood where part of the wall used to be. The smell of copper and ash tainted the air as blood ran through the streets of Madra.

Death hung over them all, but Dell kept his eyes facing forward, his mind on one thing. He had to get to that ship.

He no longer cared for Madra or the people he left behind. Many of them fought with the rebels. Others refused to fight at all.

And one girl had stood strong for them. Had fought for them.

The soldiers led them to a wagon that sat at the

bottom of the great staircase in front of the smoldering palace. Bemus put Kassander in the back. The boy stirred and lifted his head, his gaze finding Helena.

Dell set the princess in the wagon gently and climbed in. As soon as Bemus took the reins, there was no more palace. The streets of Madra whipped by, but Dell didn't see them. He didn't look into the faces of citizens who'd been roused from their beds with news of fighting at the palace.

The full moon cast a silver glow across Helena's pale skin.

Kassander spoke, but his words were lost to the sound of the wagon.

And then they heard it. Quiet at first before growing louder. Estevan Rhodipus was addressing his people.

"Citizens of Madra." His voice hung over Madra like a cloak of hope, protecting them from the evils of that night. The words carried on the breeze of Edmund's magic. This was why he'd had to stay behind.

Estevan continued. "The king is dead, but we are not without hope. To all those loyal to the crown, I tell you to stand down." His words sounded scripted, lacking the anger Dell knew was hidden underneath. Cole wouldn't risk any secret meanings. "There is a new king. I have given up my place in the line of succession to my brother, Cole Rhodipus."

He paused. "I have suffered much and do not have it in my heart to lead any longer. Cole is one of the last remaining children of my father's bloodline. In the coming days, Madra will be made stronger than ever before. Troops are being called home from wars we should not be involved in. The priesthood has been disbanded." Dell flashed back to the slaughter he'd found at the monastery. "Madra will no longer be shackled to the past by priestly traditions. We welcome a brighter future. If you are a foreigner in this land, I advise you to return to your kingdom. Madran will belong only to Madrans from this point forward."

He stopped and Dell thought he was finished until his voice began again, deeper than before. "Do not mourn my family. This night, one of my father's men murdered Princess Helena. But she did not die in vain. She sparked this change. Cole, your new king, fights for her. He fights for all of us."

Rage tore through Dell.

Kassander slumped forward, staring at his sister. "Is she truly dead?"

"No." Dell shook his head. "Your brother just pinned this entire bloody rebellion on a lie."

"Why did Estevan say those things?"

Dell's eyes flickered between Len and Kassander while his mind wandered to Estevan. He'd never liked the oldest prince. Estevan was arrogant and seemingly uncaring. But a new respect bloomed within Dell.

"Because, little prince, Estevan loves you. He did it for you."

A still breeze brought the briny air of the river delta. They'd made it. Dell blew out a long breath as he felt for a pulse again. Panic gripped him when he couldn't find it.

"Helena," he said. "Helena, you need to hold on. We're here."

They reached the Belaen ship and Mari rushed out,

jumping over the side and landing on the dock with more agility than he knew she possessed.

Kassander scrambled from the wagon. “What are we doing here?” His eyes flitted around the ships, finally landing on the dark water. “We can’t leave. What about Estevan?”

Dell ignored him as he passed Helena down to Bemus. “Mari, we need Corban, now!”

As if hearing the commotion, Corban appeared on deck. He sprinted down the wharf and dropped to Len’s side.

“I think it might already be too late.” Dell backed away, putting his hands on his head. How had he failed so miserably? The one person who’d cared for him since his mother died… and now she was leaving him too.

A familiar wrenching in his chest had him turning away, unable to watch.

Everyone held their breath.

No sound came as Corban worked over the still princess. Dell closed his eyes. Was it selfish wanting her to stay? Her parents were murdered right in front of her. Her brother would most likely be executed. The kingdom her family ruled for generations was broken.

And yet… he couldn’t let her go. He turned just in time to see her chest rise.

A scream broke free as she arched her back, echoing through the night, as if the trauma of losing everything ripped the bones right from her body.

The sound cut off abruptly, her body sagging back to the wooden planks beneath her.

“Is she going to live?” Dell asked, desperate for the answer that would start his heart again.

Corban glanced up. "I don't know. She… you may have gotten her here too late."

Mari put a hand on Corban's shoulder. "Get her on the ship. We leave as soon as Edmund arrives."

Twenty-Nine

Helena ran as smoke chased her from the rooms she'd known all her life. Destroyed, just like everything else. Her mother called to her, desperately trying to find her, but she couldn't call back as the floor tilted, sending her flying toward the dark abyss.

Helena's eyes snapped open to find herself in an unfamiliar room, smelling slightly of sweat and salt.

The sweat was probably hers. The dress she wore clung to her body with dampness. She lifted an arm to wipe sticky hair from her face, feeling the exhaustion in every movement.

Weak. She was so weak. Why?

The memories rushed in like a hurricane hurtling toward a ship at sea. And she was utterly lost to them.

"Mother," she cried.

Tears streamed down her face as if her body was emptying itself of everything she'd seen. Everything she'd done.

Where was she?

Light broke through the cracks between the rotting boards of the door. She lay on a small bed in the corner of a room with little else. Netting hung from the ceiling, dipping down over stacks of crates on the far wall.

The door rattled, and she reached for her knife, but it was no longer hidden in the folds of her skirt. She pushed herself up slowly, her muscles screaming in protest.

Light flooded the room as the door burst open. She shielded her eyes as a figure stepped closer.

Kassander. Her brother didn't smile in greeting, but the relief was clear in his eyes. "You're awake." He hesitated.

Tears welled in her eyes. At least one person hadn't been taken from her. "And you're here."

He stepped toward the bed and she reached out, pulling him the rest of the way. "I can't believe they got you out."

"It was Dell," he said, his voice muffled in her hair.

Dell. He was there too. The room swayed, and Helena pulled back. "Are we on a ship? How long have I been out?"

Kassander wasn't the one who answered.

"Over a day." Dell stood in the doorway, his gaze latching onto her face. "It's good to see you conscious, Princess."

Why the formality? She shook her head. "I'm not a princess any longer."

Dell's smile was tentative.

Helena hugged Kassander again, meeting Dell's eyes over her brother's shoulder. *Thank you,* she mouthed.

She pulled back and gripped Kassander's shoulders. "You and I now, kid. We're all that's left until we find

Quinn." She hated to think of what could have happened to Quinn. The army was in league with Cole. Did they turn on Quinn?

"Stev is still alive, Lenny," he whispered. "I know he is."

Helena didn't want to voice what she thought Cole would do to Stev, so she scooted to the edge of the bed.

A memory of pain shocked through her. The knife. She felt for the wound in her shoulder but perfectly smooth skin was all she found through the hole in her dress.

"Is this what it felt like for you every time?" she asked Dell. "Whenever Corban healed you?"

Sympathy entered his gaze. "Exhaustion? Utter weakness? A complete disbelief in what occurred?"

"That's about it."

He nodded. "Yeah. Mari explained it to me once. His magic uses your body's own energy to heal the wound. It takes a while to get it back."

Kassander stood and reached a hand out to her. She took it and pulled herself to her feet, stumbling before gaining her footing.

Kassander scrunched up his face. "You stink, Len."

A laugh burst free from Dell, but he covered it up with a cough. "Mari left some clothes for you." He pointed to a small stack of linen clothing. "I'll have someone bring a bucket of water. Sponge baths are all we have, I'm afraid. But we'll be in Bela in two days' time."

SOMEWHAT CLEAN AND FRESHLY CLOTHED, Helena found Edmund sitting on deck, his eyes scanning the direction they'd come from. He didn't look to her as she sat beside him, lowering herself with care.

She let the silence soak into her, soothing her fraying mind. The loss still hadn't quite sunk in. She'd seen it with her own eyes, her burning kingdom, but it still felt like it happened to someone else.

Finally, he spoke. "Alex is going to kill me for leaving his sister in Madra."

"Alex is the Belaen king?" she asked.

He nodded. "But there was nothing I could do. Short of tearing the palace apart stone by stone looking for where Cole hid her…"

Helena took his shaking hand in hers. "You did everything you could."

"Then why does it feel like I failed him?"

He wasn't speaking of Alex any longer. "Edmund, you didn't. Stev knew what he was doing. I would give everything to change his decision, but it was his to make."

Edmund's chin dropped to his chest, and a strangled cry rattled through his lungs.

Helena wouldn't let him give up. Not now. "My mother once told me Madra was a glass kingdom." A tear slid down her cheek. "I didn't know then she was teaching me a lesson."

Edmund's voice was so low she barely heard it. "Glass kingdom?"

Helena smiled at the memory. Her father refused to let her attend council meetings to learn about the six kingdoms, but her mother served as teacher. "Madra has always been fragile, sitting on the edge of its own destruction. Constant wars and inept rulers sent fissures through the surface. Mother told me when Madra finally shattered, it would destroy everything. Glass doesn't just break. It creates shards, weapons. And once it breaks, there's no putting it back together."

Edmund finally turned to look at her, pleading with her for something, anything to hold on to. "What kind of shard did this create? Where is our weapon?"

She broke their stare, gazing out at the rolling waters slapping the side of their ship. She sucked in a breath, the need for vengeance coming on so suddenly it shocked even her.

When she turned to Edmund once more, her eyes swirled with every emotion in each of their chests. One simple word could shape their entire future.

"Me."

Thirty

Plans rolled through Helena's mind. A light had entered Edmund's eyes at her declaration. He was with her. They may not be able to save Stev, but they could reclaim the throne.

She could make Cole pay for everything he'd done.

And she would.

As if the desire for revenge fused the pieces together, she found herself feeling whole once again. This was who she was meant to be.

Madra may have been a glass kingdom, but she was stronger than that.

She stood on deck with Dell on one side and Edmund on the other. Kassander stood at the rail, eagerly scanning the shores of Bela.

White cliffs loomed over the sea surrounded by lush green forests and a white sandy beach. The docks were not quite the bustling port of Madra, but plenty of people witnessed their approach.

Four figures stood at the end of the wharf, waiting. As

soon as the sailors tied the ship off, Edmund led them forward.

"Don't be afraid," he whispered. "Etta can be quite intimidating, but it's really her horse that's the scary one."

Dell laughed. "Her horse? You're scared of a horse?"

"You haven't met Vérité."

The woman who stepped in front of the others was not what Helena had expected. She didn't wear the long gown of other queens Helena had met. Instead, fighting leathers stretched across her small frame. Long golden hair twisted into a braid that hung over one shoulder, but no crown sat nestled in the tresses.

"That's the queen?" Helena asked.

Edmund chuckled.

The queen's stern face transformed as soon as she saw Edmund and she sprinted down the wharf, throwing herself into his arms and wrapping her thin legs around his waist.

Dell raised an eyebrow and Helena looked on in shock. No formality or sense of decorum. Who was this queen?

Edmund squeezed her so tight, Helena thought the queen would explode.

"I've missed you, Edmund."

Edmund set her down. The smile on his lips didn't reach his eyes and Helena wasn't the only one who noticed. The queen touched his face.

"I'm so sorry for everything you've been through." Her tone was serious, but it didn't hold the weight it would if she knew the truths he was really carrying. She didn't know everything he'd left behind.

A man joined them, hugging Edmund just as hard as the queen had.

"Alex," Edmund said. "I need to tell you something."

"Camille is still in Madra," the man said, releasing Edmund. "I know."

"I'm so sorry."

Alex clasped his shoulder and turned to Helena and Dell. "I imagine you have stories for us."

"How did you know we were coming?" Edmund asked.

"Ara is in Cana. Near the Madran border. Apparently, the Canan ambassador rode for the border as soon as the rebellion began."

Edmund nodded as if it all made perfect sense.

"Am I the only one thinking that still doesn't explain how you knew what happened so quickly?" Helena asked.

All eyes turned to her.

The queen studied her from loose-fitting trousers to soiled tunic. "Ara is a magic wielder. She can direct her voice to be heard over a great distance."

Magic. Of course.

"Are you going to introduce us, Edmund?" the queen asked. "Or are you just going to be rude?"

Edmund wrapped an arm around Helena. "This is Princess Helena of Madra."

The queen's eyes widened.

Edmund continued, pointing to Kass. "Prince Kassander."

"Edmund," the king said his name as a curse. "Are we to have Madran forces showing up on our shores demanding their return?"

"The only way I go back," Helena started. "Is to reclaim what's mine."

The queen smiled. "I like her."

Edmund introduced the others as another man ran toward them. He launched himself at Edmund, thumping him on the back. "Never leave again," the young man said. Dark curls flopped into his eyes.

"Hey, Ty," Edmund said. "Meet the prince and princess of Madra." Edmund looked to Helena. "This is Prince Tyson.

Tyson shot them a grin. "Ty is fine." He turned back to Edmund. "Matteo is here too."

A shadow crossed over Edmund's face, and Helena slipped her hand into his. As they were led down the docks, she leaned in. "You okay?"

"I used to think I loved Matteo. When I left for Madra, it hurt. But not like this. Not like Stev. I can't tell any of them about Stev. I can't have them looking at me as if I'm broken. Especially Matteo."

"You're not broken, Edmund."

She only wished she could feel that way herself.

Matteo greeted them, not meeting Edmund's eyes, and then the royal family led them through the village. No guards followed them. The people smiled as they passed, but none bowed. No beggars sat on street corners. Elderly folk did not live in shacks at the edge of town. It was as if the village was frozen in time, untouched by poverty or strife.

But Helena knew that wasn't true. They'd fought for what they had. The queen who looked more like a warrior had risked everything to give her people their freedom.

Why couldn't Helena do the same?

She glanced back over her shoulder to where the sea could be seen between the squat buildings and thatched roofs. Madra was out there, across the expanse. Her people went on with their lives now under the rule of the wrong brother.

And she would fight for them.

Cole Rhodipus didn't know what was coming for him.

I hope you've enjoyed Glass Kingdom. The story continues in Glass Princess, available online!

M. Lynn is a USA Today bestselling author of love. Yes, love. Whether it be YA romance (Under Michelle MacQueen), NA romance, or fantasy romance, she loves to make readers swoon.

The great loves of her life to this point are two tiny blond creatures who call her "aunt" and proclaim her books to be "boring books" for their lack of pictures. Yet, somehow, she still manages to love them more than chocolate.

When she's not sharing her inexhaustible wisdom with her niece and nephew, Michelle is usually lounging in her ridiculously large bean bag chair creating worlds and characters that remind her to smile every day - even when a feisty five-year-old is telling her just how much she doesn't know.

See more from Michelle MacQueen and sign up to receive updates and deals!

www.michellelynnauthor.com

Acknowledgments

For some reason, this was one of the easiest books I've ever written. Dell and Helena came to life so quickly, they just flowed. Maybe it was the time of year. I wrote it in July when I had a lot of things to look forward to. Maybe it was something else.

When I began the book, I was watching my one year old nephew every afternoon. I'd write all morning and then go look into the face of the happiest boy I've ever met. A lot of my contentment in life has to do with him and his sister. Maybe when they're older, they'll see this and know how much the time meant to me. So, thank you Evelyn and Owen. You've tied our family together in a very special way.

The my family, the success of this series wouldn't have been possible without your constant support. I like to write strong sibling relationships because I've known no other kind.

Melissa Craven, my wonderful editor, writing partner,

friend. Your constant chiseling away at the problems in this story allowed it to shine.

Patrick Hodges, my ever faithful proofreader. I'm not very good at showing my appreciation, but I hope you know how much I value our friendship.

Daqri Bernardo… you've done it again. I used to think you somehow struck gold in designing my Rapunzel covers, but now I know there isn't an ounce of luck in these covers, only talent.

Thank you sounds so empty when you can't see the emotions behind the words, but just picture me as a blubbering mess right now as I thank my readers. I am so thankful for each and every one of you. I never thought I would make it as a writer, but you've lifted me up and turned my books into bestsellers. So, from the bottom of my heart, thank you. You're wonderful. You're special. I'd be nowhere without you.

www.ingramcontent.com/pod-product-compliance
Lightning Source LLC
Chambersburg PA
CBHW030518310726
48979CB00010B/1718/J

* 9 7 8 1 9 7 0 0 5 2 7 8 7 *